£2.00

This copy of

Úna Bhán
Flaxen-Haired Rebel

Comes to UNA DHUB

with best wishes from
the Author
Patrick Devaney.

Úna Bhán, Flaxen-Haired Rebel
is a sequel to the author's critically acclaimed story
Through the Gate of Ivory

"Poet and schoolteacher turned novelist, Patrick Devaney has meticulously researched this recreation of life in 17th century Ireland, based on a true story...lively and engaging...This is a pacy informative read...If only school history books were this much fun!"

Ann Dunne, *Irish Independent*

"A vivid recreation of a distant epoch, this book combines fine storytelling with the wisdom of a sage who knows that Irish identity was always a matter of negotiation between different traditions...Its pacy narrative is at once vivacious and scholarly – the outcome of an imagination which has been chasened by a strong sense of actual historical forces."

Declan Kiberd

"Distinguished first novel, historical without being the slave of research...Stanihurst's tour of Connacht encounters echoes of the old Gaelic ways beyond the Pale and hellish realities of what is to come."

Books Ireland

"This is an Irish historical novel with tureens of history and hysteria at 9.9 on a post-Renaissnace Richter scale."

Kate Bateman, The Irish Times

Úna Bhán
Flaxen-Haired Rebel

Patrick Devaney

A Úna Bhán, mar rós i ngáirdín thú,
'S ba choinnleoir óir ar bhórd na banríona thú.
Ba cheiliúr is ba cheolmhar ag gabháil an
bhealaigh seo romham thú,
Agus is é mo chreach-mhaidne brónach nár
pósadh le do dhú-ghrá thú.

Thomás Láidir Mac Coisdealbh

ॐ

Fair Úna, you were like a garden rose,
And you were a gold candle on the queen's table.
You were merry-voiced and musical going
this way before me,
And it is my sorrowful morning-spoil that
you didn't wed your dark love.

Strong Thomas Costello
(Translated by the author)

First published 2008 by
Justin Nelson Productions
justin.nelson1@upcmail.ie

Copyright © Patrick Devaney, 2008

The author acknowledges the assistance of Cavan County Council under the 1973 Arts Act Grant in the publication of this book.

A CIP record for this title is available
from The British Library

ISBN 978-1-900913-24-9

Printed and bound in Ireland by eprint limited www.eprint.ie

Úna Bhán
Flaxen-Haired Rebel

Contents

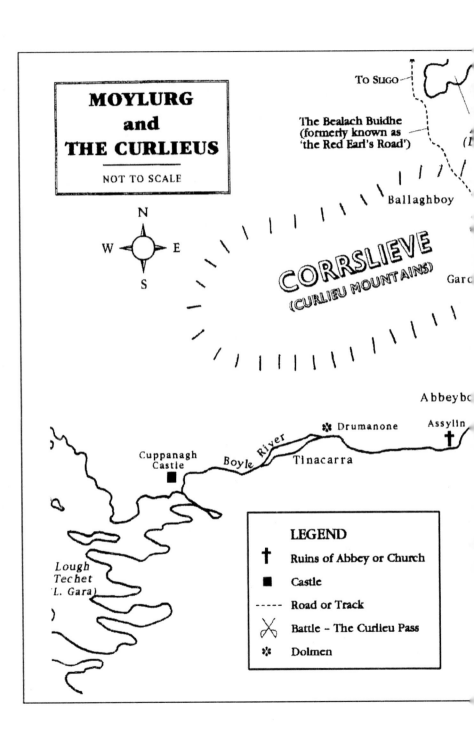

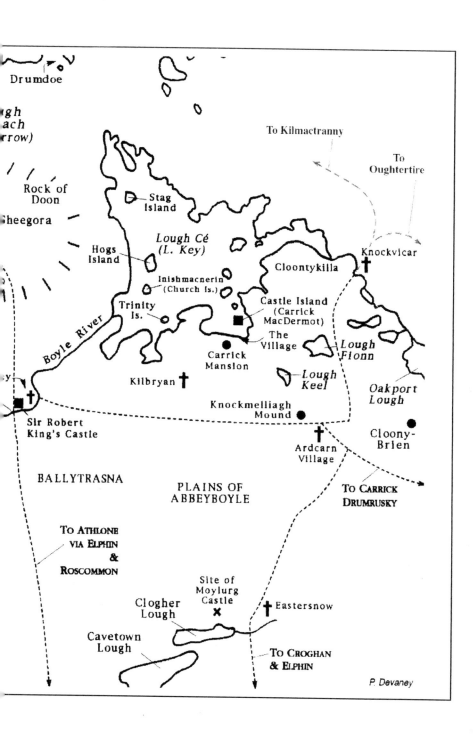

Drumdoe

gh
ach
rrow)

Rock of
Doon

Sheegora

Stag
Island

Lough Cé
(L. Key)

Hogs
Island

Inishmacnerin
(Church Is.)

Trinity
Is.

Boyle River

Cloontykilla

Castle Island
(Carrick
MacDermot)

The
Village

Lough
Fionn

Knockvicar

Carrick
Manslon

Kilbryan

Lough
Keel

Oakport
Lough

Knockmelliagh
Mound

Cloony-
Brien

Sir Robert
King's Castle

Ardcarn
Village

BALLYTRASNA

PLAINS OF
ABBEYBOYLE

To Carrick
Drumrusky

To Athlone
via Elphin
&
Roscommon

Site of
Moylurg
Castle

Clogher
Lough

Eastersnow

Cavetown
Lough

To Croghan
& Elphin

P. Devaney

Foreword & Acknowledgments

In my previous novel, *Through the Gate Of Ivory*, Úna Bhán MacDermot, though not one of the three girls wooed by the hero, was an important character. Moreover, with her refusal to conform to her society's expectations in regard to proper feminine behaviour, she became for many readers an intriguing figure, so much so that I decided to devote more time to an exploration of her personality. How would a girl who had been gently raised, the subject of Thomas Costello's love poems, become a rebel dressed in men's clothes leading an army into battle?

The present novel also covers a slightly broader period. It begins in 1636, when the Lord Deputy, Thomas Wentworth (Lord Strafford), was preparing a plantation of Connacht to boost the dwindling revenues of Charles1, and ends in 1642 with the defeat of an Irish army, assembled by Calvagh O'Conor Don at Ballintober in County Roscommon. By having Úna present in Fermanagh during the 1641 rising, in Sligo after its capture by the Irish, and at Ballintober in 1642, the atrocities committed by both sides in what became known as The Confederate Wars are touched upon, though, as might be expected, firsthand written accounts by native Irish participants are, to the best of my knowledge, unobtainable. Most of the main characters, including Úna and Daibhí, did exist but, since details about their lives are sketchy, I have used a novelist licence in fleshing out their stories.

Of the people who have been helpful in the writing of this novel, my wife, Cheryl, was always first to assess the various episodes, offering clearsighted evaluations, running off CD's and checking the proof; my sister, Christina, made detailed criticisms of style and grammar; Michael O'Donnell looked for historical errors; Michael Walsh worked out the Julian and Gregorian dates of Easter for 1642; Tom O'Dowd provided a conducted tour of Trinity Island in Lough Oughter; Sheila Crehan examined the novel sympathetically; Gerry Donagher gave information on Kilmactranny;

Mike Lennon published extracts in three editions of the *Roscommon Life* annual; Ciaran Parker gave advice on certain Gaelic names and the town of Belturbet in the 17th Century; Michael Farry cast a critical eye over some chapters; Nicola Sedgwick painted Daibhí; Catriona O'Reilly, Cavan County Arts Officer, obtained financial assistance; Jim Cleary designed the cover and retired RTE television producer Justin Nelson generously undertook the layout and publication.

Finally, there are two people who offered invaluable insights into the psychologies of the heroine and hero, my daughter, Catherine, and Kristen Eaton; without their advice Úna and Daibhí would, I feel sure, be less well-rounded characters.

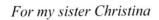

For my sister Christina

Nicola Sedwick

Daibhí Remembeing Úna

Chapter 1

You've all probably heard the story of Úna MacDermot, how she died of a broken heart after being crossed in love, but it's a lot of nonsense. I should know. I was scribe to her brother Turlough during the time she was in the full flower of womanhood and my granduncle, Philip Ballach, was the one who helped her grandfather Brian, Lord of Moylurg, to complete the Annals of Lough Key. If the writing of those annals had not been abandoned by Brian's successors there would be no doubt now about Úna's fate. As it is, all you have is rumour and guesswork, everyone trying to make her story fit an ancient pattern of father against daughter's suitor and the happiness denied the lovers in life flourishing eternally in death. Wouldn't it be great if the world were that simple?

The truth is that since all most people know of Úna is the account given of her in Thomas Costello's poem, *Úna Bán*, they are prepared to believe she was a frail, timid creature who wouldn't stand up for herself. Thomas describes her as "*a bird in a cage*" and "*a rose in a garden*". Well, a rose she may have been, but one with thorns aplenty, and, since she could sing like one, a bird she might be, but nobody could keep her long in a cage. On the contrary, she usually rode round the country dressed in doublet, breeches and jerkin, though she could play the demure damsel when it suited. If only she herself had written about her life how infinitely more gripping such an account would be than the present mishmash of half-truths and fables.

I'm sorry for going on like this. It's just that I'm now near the end of a life devoted to gathering for posterity the true account of *The Pursuit of Diarmuid and Gráinne,* and the many different versions of that tale passed down by word of mouth convinces me that unless something is written down it changes shape like smoke in a breeze. As my old teacher Muiris O'Mulconry used to assert, "What's written survives." That being the case, I've decided to set down the story of Úna MacDermot as truthfully and unflinchingly as the memory of an old man will

1

allow. Where will I begin? Maybe the year in which I first set eyes on Úna is as good a place as any.

That was 1636, when Charles 1, whom Cromwell later beheaded, was on the throne of Britain – though he claimed to be king of France and Ireland as well. The summer was good after wet weather in March and April. I had just returned from studying in our cousins' bardic school in Castlefore and was unsure of my next move. Would I head west in the hope of being employed as tutor by some noble family such as the O'Flahertys or should I stay at home to help on our land while collecting accounts of Diarmuid and Gráinne? My mother's entreaties inclined me to the latter course.

"You'll get more information here in Kilmactranny, where we're closer to Ráth Gráinne, than you'll ever get in West Connacht," she pointed out. "Why, the Barony of Tirerrill is steeped in history – Didn't the Dé Dananns defeat the Fomorians at Moytura not two miles from here? You may go further and fare worse."

Now my mother, like all her people, the MacRannells of Sheebeg, had great intelligence, so for the time being I stayed. It was while saving turf on Derrynaslieve Bog with my older brother, Philip, that Turlough MacDermot sent Rory, one of his most trusted men, to offer me a job as his scribe.

"You'll be given your keep and a fair wage," Rory told me.

"How fair?" I asked.

"You can discuss that with the master," he said. "Are you coming or not?"

"All right." I avoided Philip's eye. "As soon as we have this turf clamped, I'll be down to Cloonybrien. Maybe you'd give us a hand to speed things up?"

"Like hell I will," he grinned, before trotting off on his garron.

My father wasn't too pleased when he heard of my decision. "You've wasted three years at that school in Castlefore," he grumbled, "and now instead of pulling your

2

weight, you're off on another wild goose chase. What use is poetry to the likes of us except to give us notions above our station?"

"The O'Duigenans were ollaves and scribes long before they were scullogues," I pointed out.

"That may be so," he conceded, "but times have changed. You'll never starve with a loy in your hand, which is more than can be said for a goose quill."

Now although my father could barely read or write himself, I knew he had great respect for learning. It was just that he was getting on in years and wanted his two sons around for security.

"Look, father," I said, "apart from the New Gall, the MacDermots are still the richest people in Moylurg, and Turlough hasn't an equal for generosity."

"True enough." My father prodded the ground with his stick. "The MacDermots were Kings of Moylurg even before the Old Gall set foot in this country, but from what I hear, Turlough is now living on money borrowed from Galway merchants. They could claim his land in the morning."

"It won't happen." I spoke with the assurance of youth. "And, anyway, that's his worry. If he gives me more than my keep – which I'm sure he will – I'll see that you and mother get back what you spent on me in Castlefore."

"You're mistaken if you think I was just worrying about that." My father sounded hurt. "You're our son and we want what's best for you. But what's the use in talking? I can see that your mind's made up."

Of course he was right, for, though when the weather was fine I enjoyed lending a hand with outdoor work, the thought of spending the rest of my life planting crops, saving hay and turf and worrying if the cow had sunk in a drain appalled me.

The next morning, after embracing my sister, Eileen, and my mother – who clung to me, then kissed me and spat on my clothes for luck – I shook hands with Philip and my father and set out on foot for Cloonybrien. My legs were as limber as a hare's then, so that with a short rest near a stream to eat a griddlecake

3

and slake my thirst, I crossed the Boyle River at Knockvicar, and came in sight of MacDermot's residence by late evening.

When I approached the long thatched house flanked by half a dozen cabins, a pair of wolfhounds came charging up. Since I was armed only with a hazel stick, I expected to be torn limb from limb. Before they reached me, however, a piercing whistle brought them to heel, as obedient as spaniels. Behind them, I could see, emerging from the front door, a young man wearing a wide-brimmed hat. As he drew closer I was struck by the smoothness of his features and his fresh complexion.

"Don't mind Bran and Sgeolan," he called out in a pleasant treble voice. "They're just big *loodramawns.*"

"All the same, I'm glad they didn't jump on me," I confessed. "I'm Daibhí O'Duigenan." By this time the young man's fair countenance and sparkling blue eyes were filling me with confusion.

"Welcome to Cloonybrien, Daibhí," he smiled. "We've been expecting you all day. Turlough and his men are down at the river fishing."

"Are you his steward?" I asked, at which he broke into a peal of laughter.

"Have I said something wrong?" My cheeks were beginning to tingle.

For answer, he removed his hat, letting a mass of pale gold hair tumble to his shoulders. "I'm Úna, Turlough's sister." She grinned at my embarrassment.

"Forgive me, Mistress MacDermot." I tried to ignore the two hounds sniffing at my hands. "Your clothes – "

"Stop before you stumble in deeper!" she teased, piling up her hair with one hand and replacing her hat with the other. "Maeve has food ready for you. While you eat you can tell me all about your journey – and don't address me as Mistress MacDermot. That's far too high-sounding. Everyone calls me Úna or Úna Bhán."

ॐ

Chapter 2

On entering the house, I found myself in a long room with a fireplace at the far end, to the left of which there was a closed door. Another door in the wall on the right stood ajar, with steam and kitchen noises issuing from it. The only light, apart from the fire's blaze, came from glass windows, one in the centre of each long wall. Rushes covered the floor and there was an oak bench under both windows.

Úna announced me, whereupon the cook, Maeve, and her two young helpers, Eithne and Siobhan, greeted me warmly. A grey-haired gentleman sitting on a stool by the fire with a *cailleach* and blind harper called out "God save you" in English, to which I replied, "And you, Sir," to let him know I could speak that tongue. On hearing this, he joined Úna and me at the large table, to which Maeve and the girls carried a platter of cold mutton slices, oaten cakes, a jug of ale and three meaders from the kitchen. Úna introduced the man as Eamonn from Dunamon in County Galway. As I ate, we chatted about Castlefore and the students I had met there.

"Why did you leave?" she asked.

"I don't think I was cut out to be a poet," I confessed. "There are too many rules of metre and diction, not to mention the seven grades, from *corp* to *tochmhairc*."

"And it's all a waste of time anyway," Eamonn observed. "Who'll pay Irish rhymers when he can buy a book with the poems of Shakespeare or Spenser?"

"Don't mind Eamonn," Úna told me. "He lived too long among the Saxons."

"And proud I am to acknowledge it," he retorted. "My father sent me to Oxford because in my youth we had no university here. After that I had to go to Lincoln's Inn in the City of London to study law."

"You could have studied here to become a brehon," Una pointed out.

5

"They belong to the past, as you well know," Eamonn set down his meader of ale. "There's no gainsaying it: compared to our neighbours we're little better than barbarians."

"*Ráiméis!*" Úna gave him a withering look. "My father was educated in Trinity College and I'll warrant he was the equal of any Oxford man." I noticed there were tears in her eyes as she spoke.

"Come now!" Eamonn seemed taken aback. "No offence meant. It's just the way one acts in a disputation: parry and thrust. I've heard your father was a fine Latin scholar and had no equal when it came to the history of Moylurg and the MacDermots."

"Did you also hear that he despised those who turned their backs on their own people?" She stood up.

Eamonn didn't reply, so to ease the tension I remarked, "Muiris O'Mulconry, who taught us for the first year in Castlefore, used to say that English was like the right hand, best for smiting, but Irish was like the left, closer to the heart."

"Was Muiris really your teacher?" Úna's face changed like the sky when the sun emerges from a cloud.

"Yes," I nodded. "We were all sad when he left."

"Is he the man who is chronicler to O'Conor Don?" Eamonn enquired.

"He's their ollave," Úna corrected. "He composes poems as well as writing history. Haven't you heard the elegy he made about my father?"

"I have." I broke in. "Cúcoigcríche O'Duigenan – or Peregrine, as the New Gall call him – visited the school one day and recited it to show how much could be expressed in a single *rann*:

> *Ireland was wounded in Athlone*
> *When sickness took its fatal toll:*

6

Ill deed which made the minstrels mute,
Brian who was wounded beyond hope."

No sooner had I finished than I cursed myself for a thoughtless fool. Úna bowed her head and walked out the door.

"Leave her to herself," Eamonn whispered in English as I made to follow. "She takes those fits of weeping one minute and the next she tells us she's glad he died; that he was a tyrant who ruined her life."

I felt his readiness to reveal so much was improper. Either he wished to win my friendship or he was trying to turn me against my master's sister. How could he know that it was too late to warn me against Úna, that I had already fallen under the spell of her bright eyes and ardent spirit?

"Have you been long here?" I decided to steer the conversation onto safer ground.

"Long enough," he replied. "What I wouldn't give to be back in London!"

"What did you do there?" I replaced my *skean* in my belt.

"Why, I was a lawyer." He looked at me as if I were slow witted. "Men paid me more in one week just for drawing up deeds than I can make here in a year."

"Why did you leave?" I put on my most guileless expression.

"That's good!" he applauded. "Right to the point. I felt England was changing. The Puritans were showing their teeth at every turn – and then they fined me for not attending the Reformed service on Sundays. That took the wind out of my sails. 'Go home, Eamonn,' I told myself. 'Why sell your soul for an easy life?' So, though I love and honour the law, I took ship for Dublin – little did I realise that it would be out of the pot and into the fire."

"Can't you still practise law?" I drained my meader.

"The answer to that is yes and no: Black Tom Wentworth, the Lord Deputy, will only permit Catholics like me to practise at the minor side of the law – I can advise those whose lands are under threat from the same Black Tom but I cannot plead their cases before the bench."

Now, much as I would have liked to listen further, a full stomach and the tiredness caused by my long journey were making me drowsy, so, begging his pardon, I said I would take a walk outside.

"If you're looking for the jakes, they're by the side of the house," he remarked.

Thanking him, I stepped out into the cool evening, hoping to get a glimpse of Úna. She was nowhere in sight, however, so after a visit to the pungent jakes, I ventured into the bawn. This was a rectangular area surrounded by high, dry-stone walls, alongside which stables, cowsheds and suchlike houses had been built. An open-fronted forge stood in one corner and near it, there were lean-to huts to house fowl and another that served as a kennel. Hens foraged around stacks of hay, oats and wheat or scratched at the edges of dunghills, geese grazed the grass beneath gnarled apple trees and pigs fed noisily from a wooden trough.

As I was approaching the stable, Rory emerged.

"Ha!" he called out. "So you got here at last."

"You didn't see Úna around?" I enquired.

"She rode down to the river on Glas just a while ago." He eyed me shrewdly. "You're not chasing after her already, are you?"

"No," I lied. "It's just that she seemed upset when she left the house."

"Let me give you some advice." He rubbed his chin thoughtfully. "Don't go troubling that poor girl. She's had more than her share of misfortune from a scholar like you already."

"What scholar would that be?" I tried to sound matter of fact.

"That wild Mayo reprobate, Thomas Costello." He spat.

ଔ

Chapter 3

I was indoors listening to Eamonn trying to convince Niall Dall the Harper that the lute was the best instrument as regards lightness of melody when the sound of hoof beats reached us. "Turlough and the men!" the *cailleach,* Aine, declared, throwing more sods on the fire. Her chief tasks were to bring in turf and make up rush beds at nightfall.

In a little while we could hear strong, hearty laughter and, presently, the wolfhounds came through the door, followed by a tall man with Úna. From the plume of his broad-brimmed hat to the soles of his knee-high boots he looked every inch a chieftain. This I knew had to be Turlough, *The* MacDermot – the man who, as his father's successor, was now Lord of Moylurg.

"Here, Maeve, we've brought something for tomorrow's dinner." He held out seven or eight speckled trout on an osier withe, as proud as a boy of his catch.

"The rest of us were lucky too," Úna held out three more fish. "If it hadn't got dark we'd have made it a dozen." As she spoke I couldn't help noticing that she seemed anxious to match her brother, not just in dress but also in manly feats.

She introduced me to Turlough, who greeted me with great affability.

"I asked Ferghal O'Gara to find me a good scribe," he explained. "As you no doubt know, Ferghal is patron of Michael O'Cleirigh and the scholars above in Donegal who are writing *The Annals of the Kingdom of Ireland.* Well, Ferghal had heard tell of you from your kinsman, Cúcoigcríche – It seems Cúcoighcríche was disappointed that you left Castlefore. Anyway, you're here now, so we can put you to work on our own annals."

Not thinking it proper to mention pay, I broached the subject of where I would be sleeping.

"You can bed down over there with the men," he indicated a pile of rushes by the wall, "or, if you prefer, Aine will fix up a pallet in Eamonn's cabin. You won't mind, Eamonn?"

9

"Not at all," he replied. "We can discuss how he should go about his writing."

"So long as you don't dismiss us as barbarians!" Turlough smiled to sweeten the reproof.

By this time five fellows, who with their long hair, open doublets and ragged breeches looked like *kernes*, had come in with Rory from stabling the horses, and Turlough decided they should all join in celebrating my arrival. Accordingly, Maeve and the girls were instructed to lay out cold meats and cakes, while he himself fetched a pottle of *usquebagh* from the bedroom. Úna asked Niall Dall to play, which he did with such skill that Eamonn had to concede he might have been wrong about the lute.

"You'll sing for us, Úna. Come on!" Rory begged, whereupon she rose from the table and began to warble like a skylark "*Fol-í-ó-hó-ró*", a wistful love song I had never heard till then. Niall Dall accompanied her and we all joined in the chorus.

"Now, it's your turn, Daibhí," Úna said to me.

"I've a voice like a crow," I demurred, "but if you like, I'll recite a praise poem I made in Castlefore. It was for Brian O'Rourke, who's now in the Tower of London – His grandfather was Brian of the Ramparts."

"Oh, we knew Brian before he was imprisoned," Úna said. "Margaret, our sister, is married to his cousin, Conn."

"Let's hear it!" Turlough seemed anxious to prevent Úna's revealing too much."

Since I was tired, I don't believe my recitation was very good. Nevertheless, the company applauded as if they had just heard the greatest bard in Connacht. Begging their indulgence, I asked if I might now lie down, as I was ready to drop.

Turlough immediately directed Aine to fix up a pallet in Eamonn's cabin.

"No, Aine, don't bother," Úna said. "Daibhí and I will do it. You can light our way."

The upshot was that in a few minutes Úna and I were carrying a pallet with two *bréidín* blankets, while Aine walked ahead, shielding a candle flame with her hand. When we entered the cabin, Úna lit another candle and told Aine she could return to the house. You can imagine the thoughts that were now going through my mind, especially when Úna lay on the pallet to see if it was comfortable.

"You'll sleep like a hog on that," she pronounced before rising. "That is if Eamonn's snores don't waken you!"

I glanced at the other pallet, which was barely four feet from my own. "That'll be no problem," I said. "I'm well used to snoring after Castlefore. By the way, is your sister living near there?"

"Yes, a few hours' ride to the north." Her voice grew tense. "She couldn't wait to be married – Thought she knew what was best for me too. Well, her great husband is now out of his wits – 'Mad Con' they call him. Serves her right!"

"Aren't you being a little unkind?" I decided to speak frankly.

"No, I'm not!" she retorted. "If you knew how I was treated by my family you wouldn't be so concerned for my sister. Even my own father turned against me. And that Eamonn – I'd advise you to be wary of him."

"Why?" I asked.

"Because he's a MacDavy Burke, the same as Mairéad, Turlough's wife."

"I didn't know Turlough was married."

"Were you living in a monastery in Castlefore? I thought the whole of Connacht knows that Turlough's wife hurt herself when her horse threw her – Being a lady she of course rode sidesaddle, not astride like me. She's now living with her brother in Dunamon Castle – probably considers this place too backward."

"Didn't she see it before she married?"

"No. Turlough and Mairéad used to live with us in Carrick Mansion, our home above Lough Key. They only moved to Cloonybrien a few years ago. It was near here that Mairéad fell when they were returning from Kilbryan – Father Bernard says mass there even though the church is roofless... Eamonn pretends

11

he's here to advise Turlough about how best to retain his lands. Maybe – but you can be sure he'll report everything he sees and hears to Mairéad."

"You can rest assured he'll hear none of your secrets from me," I told her.

"Then we can be friends." She glanced around the cabin. "There's a chamber pot over there, so you won't have to go out at night. Now I'd better hurry back to the house or they'll be wondering what kept me."

When I offered her the candle she told me she could find her way in the dark. Once under the blankets I reflected on all that had occurred that day, in particular my conversation with Úna. What was troubling this bewitching girl that caused her to change so rapidly from a skylark into a hawk?

As the sounds of carousing wafted towards me on the night air, I drifted into a sleep in which Úna became Gráinne urging me to flee with her: "I put you under *geis*, Diarmuid O'Duibhne, to take me with you from this house before my father wakes up." Though I pointed out the folly of such action, I was as helpless to resist as Diarmuid had been. We travelled on foot through wild, uninhabited regions, with Turlough and his men in relentless pursuit. If we thought we had eluded them, the two hounds, Sgeolan and Bran, would pick up our scent. Finally we came to a deep wood where I knew we would be safe. As Úna was about to share my bed, Eamonn's noisy return woke me.

"Are you asleep, Daibhí?" he mumbled, half tripping over my pallet.

When I didn't answer, he threw himself fully clothed on his own pallet and was soon snoring.

ɔ෪

Chapter 4

Next morning before rising I questioned Eamonn about Mairéad, Turlough's wife. Though he was in a black mood, he told me she was now lame.

"The accident would never have happened if they had stayed in Carrick Mansion," he declared. "The poor woman's life is ruined."

"Why did they leave?" I rose on one elbow to see his face.

"How should I know?" he grumbled. "It's probably the old story, debts. They say he sold the place to Cathal Roe, his brother, to raise money."

"I suppose Úna wasn't pleased to see them leave?" I remarked.

"You may be sure of it," he sniffed. "Nothing seems to please that wildgoose – going around in man's attire! If God had created women to be our equals He'd have given them stronger bodies and keener minds, aye and stauncher spirits. At her age she should be married and raising children, not presuming to act as Turlough's steward – No wonder her father's heart was broken!"

When I tried to elicit more information, he turned to the opposite wall.

Putting on shirt, breeches, doublet and brogues, I slipped outside and made my way into a nearby grove to answer the call of nature. Returning to the cabin, I used my *skean* to shave at a basin set on a stand under the only window. While combing my hair, I noticed in the looking glass that it was going grey. Consoling myself with the thought that Finn MacCumhail had been turned grey by enchantment when still a young man, I made my way to the house. Once inside, I found men lying on piles of rushes alongside the wall, one of them snoring like a bellows. I was on the point of stealing out when Maeve emerged from the kitchen.

"Come in here." She spoke the words silently, beckoning with her hand.

13

Tiptoeing forward, I noticed Turlough sleeping on a pallet near the fireplace. His reddish-brown hair was almost bald on the crown. When I entered the kitchen, Maeve closed the door behind me then gave me a wooden spoon to stir a pot of porridge hanging over the fire.

"Where's Úna?" I enquired.

"Sleeping in the master's bedroom." She began to knead dough vigorously on the table. "It's disgraceful the way that girl behaves, drinking *usquebagh* with the men 'til she's ready to drop. If the mistress was here she'd not stand for it."

"Did Úna and the mistress not get on?" I lifted the bubbling pot off the hook and rested it on the hearth.

"They did, after a fashion – though it's easy to see that Úna isn't sorry she's gone." She put the dough in an oven, which she set on the hearth over a nest of coals, placing more coals on the lid. "Ever since the mistress went back to Dunamon, Úna has been over here for days and nights on end. Her mother should keep her in Carrick Mansion, but sure the poor woman is at her wits' ends trying to control her."

"What about her brother, Cathal Roe?" I pulled a stool up to the table.

"Neither Cathal Roe nor his wife Eleanor can do much." She placed a bowl of porridge and fresh milk before me. "Oh, Eleanor encourages her to wear a gown and smock instead of those awful breeches but she might as well save her breath. Úna tells her that she can't ride a horse in women's clothes. Ever since her father's death, she's been impossible. The only one she'll listen to," she lowered her voice, "is himself in there, and that's because he won't hear a word said against her. Oh, he's kindness itself, but – " She shook her head doubtfully.

"Rory said she was in love with a Thomas Costello." I pushed my empty bowl away.

"Don't mention that fellow!" Ignoring my raised hand, she refilled the bowl. "If anybody's turned her into a different person, it's him. Sure his people were always trying to undermine

14

the MacDermots. In the old days they were constantly fighting and raiding into Moylurg."

"Where did Úna and Thomas meet?" I pretended to eat some porridge.

"It was beyond in Bellanagare, where Cathal O'Conor has his castle. Eleanor's sister was married to Cathal – he died suddenly two years ago – and Eleanor sent Úna over to keep the widow company in her time of grief. She was probably hoping as well that a change might do Úna good. Well, things seldom turn out as we expect – "

Before she could tell me more we were interrupted by the arrival of Eithne and Siobhan from the cowhouse with frothy pails of fresh milk. Thanking Maeve for the porridge, I slipped out the back door, fearing that Turlough might not relish being caught asleep so late in the morning. Immediately I set foot in the bawn the wolfhounds came galloping up, but Rory, leading a bay horse from the stable, called them off.

"Pet them," he advised. "They won't bite."

Gingerly, I patted the big brutes, murmuring their names and to my surprise, they began to wag their tails. When I opened the gate they followed me out, delighted to have the chance to run free. My head was buzzing with what Maeve had told me about Úna's drunkenness, so, on impulse, I decided to wander by the nearby cabins rather that return to Eamonn's. Picking my way by upturned creels, ricks of turf, staring children, goose houses and tethered garrons, I ran into an old man wearing a torn grey doublet, white frieze breeches and a blue bonnet, who was carrying a bundle of firewood. When we had conversed for a short while, I learned that Art – for that was his name – had been *reachtaire* or chief steward to Turlough when he was living in Carrick Mansion. He was now too infirm to run the household, but Turlough allowed him to remain in a cabin and saw that he didn't go hungry.

"Who is *reachtaire* now?" I enquired.

"Nobody, unless it's Rory – " he grinned, "or his sister! Oh, that Úna keeps them all on their toes when she's around –

15

and more power to her! Sure she has a better head on her shoulders than any man."

He invited me in for a meadar of ale; so, leaving the dogs to roam, I entered the dark, tidy cabin. As we took turns drinking from the same vessel, he told me about life in Moylurg when Turlough's grandfather, Brian, had been alive. In those days Queen Bess was on the throne and her Lord Deputy was dividing Connacht into shires. Brian was a warrior, scholar and builder – It was he who had built Carrick Mansion. After the defeat of O'Neill and O'Donnell at Kinsale, Brian's son, Brian Oge, had been sent to Trinity College with a view to turning him into a loyal Protestant, but, thank God, that hadn't happened.

From what he told me I gathered that Cathal Roe had been living further east, near Carrick Drumrusky, at the time of his marriage, while the rest of the family, including, Úna, Turlough, their sisters, Margaret and Honora, and their parents, had been resident in Carrick Mansion by Lough Key.

It was my great good fortune to have met Art, for, later that day, after a dinner of grilled trout, watercress and oaten cakes, Turlough decided to find out the extent of my learning.

When we were alone at the table, except for Eamonn, who was smoking a long-stemmed clay pipe, he asked me, "Why is our territory known as Moylurg?"

"That's because its full name is Moylurg an Dagda, the Plain of the Track of the Dagda."

"Good. And how did Lough Key get its name?"

"It was named after the hag Key whom Oisin befriended. She turned into a beautiful woman and brought him with her to *Tír na nÓg.*"

"That's one explanation, but our father, God rest him, always maintained it was called after Key, Nuada's druid, who drowned there after the Battle of Moytura. Still, you're not wrong. Now, who defeated the English at the first Battle of the Curlew Pass?"

"Your father's kinsman, Conor Oge MacDermot, Brian Oge O'Rourke and – "

"Yes?" he leaned forward, ready to pounce.

Remembering what Art had told me, I paused as if considering: "People say it was Red Hugh O'Donnell, but he and his men were camped at Dúnaveragh, up beside Lough Arrow, while the battle was taking place."

"That's it!" He clapped me proudly on the back." Cúcoigcríche was right: you're a true O'Duigenan. As soon as I purchase some folio paper we can set you to work."

☙

"MacDermot's Castle", Lough Key
Photo; Conor Dowling

Chapter 5

Before I could begin any writing, however, we had unexpected visitors. The following morning Úna and I were heading for the nearby lough, she on Glas, her fine grey mare, and I on Banbawn, a sturdy little garron Rory had given me. When we had travelled about a mile, we saw three men on big English horses approaching from the direction of Knockvicar. There was something about the strangers that filled us with unease, either because of their dark clothes or the way they cantered abreast, as if they owned Cloonybrien and we were trespassers.

"Can you tell us where MacDermot lives?" the oldest of the three, demanded in English. He was a tall, long-faced gentleman with piercing eyes and thin cruel lips, armed like his companions with a sword and saddle pistols.

"What do you want with MacDermot?" Úna made her voice sound deeper.

"That's our concern, young fellow." The man looked her up and down with disdain. "Just direct us to his house."

"I will when you answer my question," Úna replied, whereupon one of the others, a big, florid-faced ruffian, drew his sword.

"Have a civil tongue in your mouth, Teige, or it'll be cut out," he growled.

"If you won't tell us what you want with MacDermot, how do we know that you don't intend him harm?" I heard myself demur.

"By Gad, he's right," the older man conceded. "Put up your sword, Richard. We've come to make him an offer for some lands in Keadue."

"And we'll pay good money," the third man – who, from his tall stature and similarity of features, was almost certainly his son – added.

"You'll be wasting your time," Úna observed. "He has no land for sale."

"Let that be our worry." The older man eyed her suspiciously. Before he could question her, however, she turned her mare around.

"Follow us," she directed, and we trotted off, with the three strangers keeping close on our heels.

"You shouldn't have intervened," she told me in Irish. "I knew who they were all along. It's the two Cootes and their steward, Richard Lawrence – the bodach who drew his sword."

"You didn't expect me to let him run you through?" I protested.

"I don't need anyone's protection!" She glared at me then broke into a smile. "Sometimes you have to match the arrogance of the New Gall or they'll trample all over you."

Since Úna decided to enter the kitchen through the rear door so that she could overhear what the visitors had to say to Turlough, I stayed with Rory, who was stabling the horses.

"What do you think the Cootes want?" I pretended not to know.

"Is it those two?" he snorted. "Well, the curse of God on every last one of their seed and breed. Lawrence must have told them that the master was over in Galway recently. Did you ever notice how scaldcrows turn up when they see a chance to fill their craws? They must think he's short of money."

"Where do they live?" I asked.

"They've a big castle on the Suck, below Dunamon, and another in Jamestown, on the Shannon, and that's not all." He tied the reins of Richard's horse to a post. "They have iron works in Arigna, near Keadue – that's probably where they came from today – but do you think they'd let a single Catholic inside the doors? No, we're the wild Irish Papists, fit only for the bogs and mountains. Old Sir Charles for all his reading of the bible is a greedy scaldcrow, and Young Sir Charles is a bad egg out of a bad nest. Between them and Sir Robert King over in Abbeyboyle they won't be content till they get their claws on every last acre in Moylurg."

When Maeve told me later that Rory was from East Breifne, where his family's lands near Lough Ramor had been given to planters during the time of King James, I understood his bitterness. As it was, I put it to him that my father had always spoken well of Sir Robert.

"He's not as bad as the Cootes," he conceded, "but don't be fooled by that. He has all the lands of Boyle Abbey and everything the monks owned in Lough Key. Why do you think Turlough moved from there? He didn't want to be reminded every day of what our people had lost."

Leaving Rory to get on with his work, I returned to the cabin. Eamonn was out, so to while away the time I composed a ballad set in the time of the ancient Fenians. It related how three foreign warriors hoping to enter Finn's dún on the Hill of Allen were met by a youth who challenged them to combat. The youth attacked so bravely that the oldest of the warriors exclaimed:

"If this be how their young men fight,
Who'll withstand their champions' might?"

Instead of waiting to find out, the warriors took to their heels. The youth was invited to a feast in the dun. There he revealed to the Fenians that 'he' was really the goddess Macha, who had come to save them from their enemies.

By the time I was finishing the last rann, Eamonn arrived. He had been with Turlough during the Cootes' visit, but beyond saying that no land had been sold, would reveal little. I told him about our own meeting with the Cootes, after which I recited the ballad to see if it would pass muster.

"It's not bad," he took a pinch of snuff then, eyes watering, continued "but you should read the 'Chanson de Roland.' Now, that's an account of heroic deeds."

Despite this judgement, he proclaimed to everybody at our evening meal that I had composed a ballad. Turlough, who was sitting at the head of the table, toying with his food, looked at me from under his hat brim. It was plain that whatever had passed between him and the Cootes was still on his mind.

21

"Aren't you going to recite it, Daibhí?" Úna, hatless, her hair like a candle flame, called out from the other end of the table.

"It's just a half-made thing," I demurred. "When it's finished properly, I'll let you all hear it."

"That's not your choice," Turlough spoke sharply. "Let's hear it now."

Since there was no escape from this direct command, I began to declaim in mock-heroic style. At first there was silence, though Úna, followed by Turlough, quickly perceived what the ballad was about. When I came to the combat a smile of childish delight lit up Úna's face and Turlough, noting her enjoyment, began to smile too. By the time I had finished even the *kernes* were grinning at the unexpected outcome.

"Bravo!" Turlough took two gold sovereigns from his purse and handed them to me. When I told him I didn't expect payment, he said, "We've always rewarded our poets. Take them."

It would be false to pretend that I didn't delight in my triumph for at that moment a new world was opening before me. This was a poem I had composed especially for the MacDermots. The way it had been received showed that I could now hope to become their *ollave*, instead of a mere scribe. My years in Castlefore hadn't been wasted. From this day on I would be called on to recite at their feasts and they would reward me lavishly with gold.

That evening Úna walked with me to the cabin. There was an excitement in her voice as if together we were about to embark on some great adventure. Years later, however, I was to ask myself if that ballad of mine had planted an idea in her head that led to her undoing.

CB

Chapter 6

The next day being Sunday, Úna, Turlough, Eamonn and I set out early on horseback to attend mass in Kilbryan church, which lies south of Lough Key, some little way beyond Carrick Mansion. As we approached the lough I got my first glimpse of Carrick MacDermot, the MacDermots' ancient fortress, sitting on its rock a short distance out in the water. Ahead of us on a hill stood Carrick Mansion, where the family now lived. This two-storied, thatched house was surrounded by a hazel palisade, which, here and there, had taken root. For me, the brown thatch, lime-white walls and green hazels offered a most pleasing spectacle. At the foot of the hill there was a village known as *Baile na Carraige.* This was little more than a few dozen cabins sprawled haphazardly beside the shore.

When we drew near the village Turlough suggested that Úna and I should ride ahead to the mansion while he and Eamonn visited some of the cabins.

"Why can't I come with you?" Úna protested.

"Because Father Bernard won't be pleased to see you in doublet and breeches," he explained.

"If they were good enough for Joan of Arc they should be good enough for any woman," she pouted but Turlough only laughed.

When we reached Carrick Mansion, Niall the *Reachtaire* took our horses to the stable, while Bridgeen, who had been Úna's nursemaid, welcomed us warmly. She then led us into the oak-panelled Great Hall, where Úna's mother, Lady Margaret, and her sister, Honora, were sitting by a massive stone fireplace. They rose with uneasy expressions when we entered. Lady Margaret was an aristocratic-looking widow dressed in black. She had Úna's oval face, blue eyes and fair hair but Honora was frail and brown haired, with a pale complexion, except for a bright rose in each cheek.

"Welcome home, Úna," Lady Margaret said as Honora watched silently.

23

"This is Daibhí O'Duigenan, Turlough's scribe," Úna introduced me. "I'm going to change my clothes."

Leaving Honora to look after me, Lady Margaret followed Úna upstairs.

"Will I get you something to eat?" Honora spoke timidly.

I assured her that I wasn't hungry then asked about the rest of the household. She told me that Cathal Roe and his wife Eleanor were attending Divine Service in Boyle Abbey because Sir Robert King would expect them there, that Brian and Hugh, their children, were with their nursemaid, Orlaith, and that Teige, her brother, was staying in Croghan with Eleanor's family, the O'Mulloys.

I was about to bring up her sister Margaret who was married to Mad Con when angry voices from upstairs reached us. Úna was accusing her mother of having moved her clothes while she was gone and Lady Margaret was explaining that she had simply tidied the wardrobe.

"You're lying!" Úna screamed. "You were looking for *gafann*."

"Keep your voice down," Lady Margaret pleaded. There was the sound of a door being hastily shut then the discord continued, muffled voices rising and falling. Poor Honora seemed shamed by the quarrel, so to distract her, I recounted our meeting with the Cootes.

"Didn't they know Úna was a girl?" she asked in surprise.

"If they did, they didn't reveal it," I said. "It all happened very quickly."

We were talking about her father Brian Oge's years in Trinity when Úna and her mother came downstairs with strained looks on their faces, Úna looking beautiful in a green gown tied with a *crios*.

"Isn't the gown I'm wearing all right for mass?" Úna appealed to me.

"I told her she should wear this one out of respect for her father's memory." Lady Margaret held out a black gown.

"You look like the Dé Danaan princess, Niamh Chinn Óir," I assured Úna, "but your mother's right."

For a moment it seemed that her glare would wither me, then in a calm, pitiless voice she said, "Why should I mourn for my father when he sided with that woman against me?"

"That's a fine way to speak about your parents before a visitor," Lady Margaret reproved.

"He always treated you as his favourite," Honora pointed out.

"Be quiet!" Úna commanded. "You always take mother's side."

"With your fair hair, Úna, I'm sure you'll look even lovelier in black." Throwing caution to the wind, I met her angry gaze. "And, anyway, if we don't hurry, Turlough will leave without us."

This intervention won the day. Úna went back upstairs, while her relieved mother pointed out the portraits of the children's grandparents that flanked the fireplace: Brian, Lord of Moylurg, on the left and Maeve, daughter of O'Conor Sligo, on the right. She also mentioned that her own grandfather was the second Earl of Clanricarde.

"You're a Burke then," I observed.

"No, a De Burgo," she corrected. "My people come from Derrymaclachny."

Before she could tell me more, Úna reappeared, and truly, if a black gown became anyone, it was this shapely young woman. Over the gown she was wearing a black mantle with a hood that could be pulled forward to cover her hair.

Not wishing to delay further, I bade farewell to Honora and Lady Margaret, promising them that we would remind Turlough to come back for dinner.

"Now, wasn't I right?" I exclaimed, hurrying Úna out the door.

"Oh, men are always right!" she pouted, then leaned on my arm as we picked our way over the mucky, hoof-scored ground to the stable. Once there, she had to endure the further indignity of sitting sideways behind me on Banbawn.

Waving to Niall and Bridgeen, we rode out through the palisade entrance. From the hilltop there was a fine view of the lough with its wooded islands and the blue-green hills rising beyond its further shore. Úna pointed out Inishmacnerin, which was occupied by Canons Regular till King Henry suppressed the monasteries, and Trinity Island, where monks lived till the time of King James. Both of these holy places had been protected by the MacDermots, but now belonged to Sir Robert King. The only remaining monk was a Cistercian, Father Bernard, who lived in Carrick MacDermot. When she had finished talking, I decided to again risk offending her.

"Before we go to the village, Úna, there's one question I just have to ask. Can you tell me what *gafann* is?"

"You were eavesdropping!" she struck me on the back.

"Well, you were eavesdropping yourself on Turlough and the Cootes."

"That's different: Turlough's my brother."

"Look, Úna, forgive me. I just couldn't help overhearing."

"You should have blocked your ears."

"If you don't wish to answer – "

"Oh, you'll find out anyway. It's a plant that helps you sleep. If you took too much you might never wake up – or so mother thinks."

Chapter 7

Rain began to fall as we trotted towards Kilbryan after Turlough and Eamonn. My clothes were soon damp and the hay-filled cushion that served as a saddle chafed my thighs but I was as happy as Oisín riding to Tír na nÓg with the gold-haired Niamh. How could I on the day I left home with only a hazel stick and griddlecake have foreseen this turn of Fortune's wheel? The beautiful girl behind me might not think me worthy to be her suitor, but I was still young enough to believe that even a poor scholar like me could turn into a prince. Should such metamorphosis be unlikely, hadn't Úna and I still something in common? Didn't we both wish to cast off the lives into which we'd been born, I to exchange the spade for the goose quill, she the satin gown for a frieze doublet?

"Do your mother and Honora not go to mass?" I asked just to hear her speak.

"No," she replied. "Mother tells everybody she must stay home because Honora is ailing. The truth is she doesn't wish to mix with the ragamuffins from the Plains and those vulgar people from the village."

"She was friendly to me," I remarked.

"That's because she's afraid you might write a satire," she said. "Isn't that what poets do when they're displeased with their welcome?"

"So that's why you've been so welcoming!" I teased.

For answer she struck me lightly on the ribs and we both laughed. Despite her habit of turning against those who curbed her, she was at heart a child.

As we drew near the roofless church we could see a group of men and women standing outside. Some ragged fellows immediately hurried forward, walking alongside Turlough's horse with doffed bonnets as they greeted him like a conquering hero. A barefooted scullogue took Banbawn's reins, leading him over to a whitethorn, where he tied the reins to a branch.

Before I could help Úna to dismount, a powerfully built fellow with a mane of glossy black hair strode up. Placing his hands on Úna's waist, he lifted her lightly off the garron's back. When I began to protest, he told me not to fret, that it was to save her shoes from the muck. Judging by the smile on her face I knew this had to be her admirer, Strong Thomas Costello.

Instead of setting her down, Costello carried Úna over to where Turlough was waiting with Eamonn. I expected Turlough to reprimand him but he merely nodded, then ushered his sister inside followed by Eamonn and me. The congregation parted to let us reach the top of the stark, rectangular church, where Father Bernard in a black cassock and white surplice, flanked by two bare-footed boys, smiled at us. Behind the priest, there was a stone altar placed under the gable window. The window was set in an arched recess and had four vertical openings that might formerly have held glass.

Since there were no pews we all stood while Father Bernard read the mass in Latin. Rain continued to fall lightly but nobody seemed to mind so engrossed were they in everything that was taking place. After the consecrated bread had been distributed Father Bernard, standing with his back to the altar, addressed us in the strong, though kindly, accent of a ploughman.

"Beloved people," he began, "it pleases me that so many of you have travelled here today despite bad weather, long distances and the danger of being reported to our enemies. Some of your grandparents will remember when there were seven churches in northern Moylurg. Now we have only these four walls, while the Lutherans hold their service inside the sacred walls of Boyle Abbey and make us pay tithes to support their rector. Yet, it doesn't matter about stones and timber. Jesus said, 'Where two or three are gathered together in my name, there am I in their midst.'

"We are living in dangerous times. Some of you may have heard the rumour that the king's surveyors will soon be measuring the entire province of Connacht so that he can give our land to the New Gall. Maybe this is a punishment from God for our transgressions: couples living together without the blessing of a priest; children not being baptized; people attending the Lutheran services to safeguard their property – It goes on and on. You all know that in these times of trial we must remain faithful to the One True Church or we will lose more than land and flocks: 'What doth it profit a man if he gain the whole world and suffer the loss of his immortal soul?'"

I glanced at Úna to see if she was taking this as a criticism of Cathal Roe but the hood covered most of her face; beyond her Turlough stood hatless, his expression inscrutable.

"But you mustn't think that the Church is indifferent to your temporal welfare," Father Bernard continued. "Our good bishop, Doctor Egan, a fugitive in his own diocese, has told me that he intends to write to the Holy Father in Rome to beg him to intercede for us with Queen Henrietta Maria, who is a devout Catholic. He hopes she will ask her husband, Charles, our headstrong king, to remedy this unbearable evil that threatens us. In the meantime we must all pray that God, who delivered the Israelites from the hands of their oppressors, will deliver us too.

"To conclude, I want to remind parents to bring their children to me this evening for instruction in the faith, otherwise they may live to see them lured one day into the fold of Luther. God bless you, my good people. Now let us pray."

When mass ended, Turlough remained behind to talk to Father Bernard, while Eamonn, Úna and I shuffled out with the rest of the congregation. Thomas was waiting by the door. Without a word of explanation he and Úna went off hand in hand as if they had no awareness of everybody watching.

"Will someone tell me what she sees in that vagabond?" Eamonn sniffed, but I was too downcast to answer.

"Look! They're heading for the oak grove," he exclaimed. "Wait till Turlough learns of this: I don't think that fellow came here to pray."

By this time people, hearing him talk in English, were looking at us with curiosity.

"Maybe they intend to walk back to Carrick Mansion," I spoke in Irish for fear of being thought a foreigner. "I'll ride after them."

The rain had stopped by the time I had picked my way through the crowd over to the whitethorn, turned the saddle cushion over and retightened the girth. Without waiting for Eamonn or Turlough I set off. Úna and Thomas were no longer in sight, so I concluded that they had entered Derreendarragh, as the oak grove was known.

On reaching the grove I dismounted and tied Banbawn to a tree. The only sound was the singing of thrushes, blackbirds and finches and the ticking of a wren. I went forward on foot, my brogues making no noise on the carpet of old leaves. The odour of damp clay was strong in my nostrils. Presently I spied the two lovers standing under a tree, Úna's fair head on Thomas's shoulder, his arms about her in a passionate embrace. For some reason the words of the song she had sung on my first evening in Cloonybrien came rushing back:

> *One day that I was in yon trees*
> *I saw a maid with glad, slow eyes,*
> *Stick in hand and she fragrant, lithe.*
> *Oh, she's my inmost heart's delight.*

The two were so still, so unaware of anything but themselves that I left them there and made my way silently out of the grove. That should have ended my passion for Úna, but it didn't. I was under *geis* like Diarmuid with Gráinne, doomed to love her no matter what would befall me.

Chapter 8

"Where's that sister of ours?" Cathal Roe asked on coming into the Great Hall with his wife Eleanor. Though not as tall as his brother, he was a powerfully built, red-haired man whose beard was neatly trimmed in the English fashion. As he spoke, Eleanor, a plump, fair haired young woman, dressed in a fringed green cloak and broad beaver hat, hurried over to claim her children from Lady Margaret, who was sitting at the end of the table with Terence on her lap and little Brian beside her. I was seated on her left, facing Turlough and Eamonn across heaped platters of roast veal and oaten cakes.

"Honora wasn't feeling well," Lady Margaret explained. "I told her to lie down."

"I was asking about Úna." Cathal Roe shook hands with Eamonn.

"She's on her way back from Kilbryan," Turlough told him. "This is my scribe, Daibhí. He's related to the Kilronan O'Duigenans."

I rose and Cathal Roe shook my hand. "How come Úna didn't return with you?" He addressed his brother, whose worn leather jerkin, saffron doublet, shaven face and down-curving moustache were in sharp contrast with his own well-kept appearance.

"She decided to walk." Turlough looked uncomfortable.

"I see." Cathal Roe smiled grimly then he and Eleanor went upstairs.

During this time Bridgeen and three servant girls were carrying in bowls of onions, leeks and *praiseach bhuí*, jugs of buttermilk, flagons of claret and, something I had never seen till then, a *ciseán* of roots called potatoes. Lady Margaret got Bridgeen to mix one of these with butter, which she then proceeded to feed to her grandchildren.

We were all enjoying the rich fare, Cathal Roe at the head of the table, with Eleanor on his right, when Úna came in with Daithleen, the family's spaniel.

31

"So you're back!" Cathal Roe observed.

"Yes, brother, I'm back," she replied.

"What kept you?" he demanded.

"I was enjoying a walk with Thomas." She lifted the delighted Brian, a curly headed two-year old, in her arms.

"I thought I told you to have nothing more to do with that fellow," Cathal Roe was controlling his temper.

"You're not my father!" Úna retorted. "Do I tell you that you shouldn't attend the Lutheran service in Abbeyboyle?"

"That's an entirely different matter," Cathal Roe huffed. "I'm doing that to keep these lands safe for all of us."

"How come father never thought of that?" Úna put Brian down and went upstairs.

"I'd go easy on her," Turlough advised. "The more we warn her against Costello the more she'll want to see him."

"Why don't you discuss this at a later time?" Eleanor begged Cathal Roe, after turning the children over to their nursemaid, Orlaith.

"Yes." Lady Margaret concurred. "We don't want to have our Sunday dinner spoiled."

Her two sons looked at each other but did not say anything. In a little while Úna came downstairs dressed again in doublet and breeches. Instead of sitting in the empty space beside her mother, she squeezed in between Eleanor and me so that I had to move further down. We ate for a while in silence then Lady Margaret asked Eamonn if he intended to stay in Ireland.

"What else can I do now, Lady Margaret?" he replied. "There's no place for a recusant in England. If Turlough finds me of use I'm glad to assist him."

"When you say you're a recusant, do you mean that the fines for not attending the Protestant services are rigorously enforced?" she asked.

"I suppose it's much like here," he explained. "In one place they are and in another they turn a blind eye. But so long as your son requires my advice, I'll be honoured to guide him through the thickets of the law."

"Much good that will do," Turlough remarked. "Did you see what happened last year in Abbeyboyle? Wentworth told the jurors that as far as law was concerned, His Majesty's title to the lands of Connacht was plain. If they didn't find for him he would be within his rights to seize their estates outright."

"Father Bernard said that the king's surveyors will begin work soon," I plucked up the courage to add.

"And you can be sure they will," Eamonn nodded in agreement. "When it comes to the law the English could build a nest in your ear and rob it again."

"Isn't that all the more reason for us to make friends with them?" Cathal Roe fingered his cup of claret.

"The only reason they treat us like spaniels is because we are spaniels," Turlough declared. "If we don't stand up to them they won't leave us enough land to dig ourselves a grave in."

"That kind of talk could get us all dispossessed," Cathal Roe warned.

"Isn't it better to fight than to live year after year in dread of being dispossessed? Úna asked.

"You don't know what you're talking about," Cathal Roe sniffed. "I suppose that's what that Mayo woodkerne told you."

"I'm well able to think for myself." Úna kept her temper. "You're convinced that because I'm a girl I've no understanding of what's going on around us. Don't you recall that Maeve, Queen of Connacht, led an army against Ulster and that Joan of Arc drove the English out of France? Oh yes, and what about Gráinne O'Malley who with her Mayo warriors fought the English on land and sea and sailed to Greenwich to demand justice from Queen Bess?"

"Who's been filling your head with those fairy tales?" Cathal Roe scoffed.

"Believe it or not, it was our father!" Úna smiled triumphantly. "He didn't seem to think me as empty headed as you do."

"He didn't expect you to go round the country dressed like that either," Cathal Roe mocked. "And if you had so much

33

respect for him, why did you refuse to travel to Athlone for his funeral?"

"Now, Cathal!" Lady Margaret objected.

"I didn't go because you and mother turned him against me before he died." Úna's voice choked.

"That's not true," Cathal Roe declared as Úna, leaving her food half eaten, rushed distracted out the door.

"Daibhí," Turlough said, "maybe you'd go after her? She might listen to you."

Throwing a cloak about my shoulders and taking another for Úna I hurried from the Great Hall. There was no sign of Úna in the nearby sheds or cabins; then I encountered Niall, who told me she might be down at the village. On descending the hill, to approach the village, I spied far away on my left Daithleen, the spaniel, racing about under bushes. Hurrying over I found Úna sitting on a rock near the water, indifferent to the rain falling on her bare head. She did not look up as I approached.

"I brought you a cloak," I said, draping it about her shoulders. The next moment my heart almost stopped. Blood was flowing from a cut on her left arm and dripping onto the gravel.

Chapter 9

I once saw a finch my brother had grazed with his slingshot. The little bird that a few moments before had been flying through the air, beautiful and lively, sat on the ground trembling, its wing drooping, its bright eye dulled. As I looked at Úna sitting there dazed and bedraggled I thought of the wounded finch. Then I noticed the skean in her hand and it jolted me out of my trance.

"What have you done?" I cried, snatching the skean away.

She looked at me hollow eyed but did not answer. Quickly I gathered a handful of moss and told her to keep it pressed on the wound. Next I tore strips from my shirtsleeve, which I bound around the moss to keep it in place. As I worked Úna began to sob quietly.

"Why did you cut yourself?" I asked.

"I'm no good," she whispered. "You should have let me die."

"What would Thomas think if he heard talk like that?" In my pity for her I completely forgot my jealousy. "You're the 'maid with glad, slow eyes' that he worships."

"Father told me he would rather see me lying dead than married to him," she replied. "That's why I refused to go to his funeral – Now I truly wish I had."

"People say and do wild things in anger," I pointed out. "Try standing up."

Holding her right arm, I raised her to her feet. Immediately her legs began to give way so that I had to put my arm about her waist to support her. Here I was half embracing the loveliest girl I had ever laid eyes on and, instead of joy, my heart was filled with pity.

"You must think bad of me for hating my father," she said. "He used to tell me I was his princess, but that was before I saw through him."

"What did you see?" I asked.

"That he was weak and unworthy to be chief of our people." She pulled free of my arm. "He had turned into a Teige-of-Both-Sides."

"He wasn't the only one of our leaders that did that." I picked up her skean and put it in my belt. "Nearly every family had sons or brothers who fought for the Queen in the last war."

"I didn't hate my father." She ignored my words. "But he filled my head with heroic tales – And then he wanted to betroth me to one of the New Gall."

"Who would that be?" I didn't hide my surprise.

" John King, Sir Robert's eldest son." She smiled bleakly. "Do you know that his grandfather, Sir John, who just died, tricked O'Conor Don out of his seat in parliament and that his father now owns all the land that belonged to Boyle Abbey? Thomas can see that the New Gall will take everything we own unless we unite against them but when I told father that, he said, 'It's easy for the likes of him; he has nothing to lose.' And Cathal Roe backed him up. He's another Teige-of-Both-Sides, aping the foreigners when he should be upholding our ways."

"Why don't we head back to the house?" I was fearful that her arm might still be bleeding.

She grimaced. "I'm not going back there. Look at Eleanor; just my age and already she has two children and another on the way. That's what my father had in mind for me. He wanted to use me as a pawn to save his inheritance; it didn't matter about my happiness. How could he have changed like that?"

"Would John King not be a good husband then?" I asked.

"Oh, good enough," she conceded. "If that's what I wanted. He's a student in Cambridge and next year he'll be studying in Lincoln's Inn. Father always said lawyers aren't to be trusted – Why then did he want me to marry one?"

"Did you ever meet John King?"

"Yes. Last summer he and his brothers, Henry and Robert, came to their new Abbeyboyle castle – they live in Baggotrath Castle in Dublin – and father invited them here to go fishing.

Their mouths fell open when they saw the poverty of the villagers, but still they enjoyed themselves. I suppose they told all their friends when they went back to Dublin about their sojourn among the Wild Irish. I'm not saying that John and his brothers were uncivil, just that their ways are different from ours – Can you see me living in a castle, wearing fine gowns, with a host of servants at my beck and call? "

All this time light rain had continued to fall, so I urged her, if she didn't wish to return to Carrick Mansion, to seek shelter in the village, where somebody could tend her arm. Finally, she consented, provided I would tell Lee, the village healer, she had been cut while we were pretending to fight with skeans. Though it seemed a most childish lie, I was too fearful that the wound might rankle to refuse her request. As a result, from that time on we grew closer, sharing secrets like two conspirators. What I didn't realise was that I had begun to follow a will-o'-the-wisp which in years to come would lead me into unimagined dangers.

Lee's mud and wattle cabin was much like Art's, only more cluttered, with shelves bending under the weight of jars of simples and herbal juices. When the door was pulled shut the interior was left in semidarkness, there being but one tiny parchment-covered window. Sean Lee was a friendly, voluble man of middle years, while his wife Nora reminded me of my mother. She fussed over Úna, telling her to bring Daithleen inside but Úna, concerned for the cat dozing by the turf fire, said he would find his own way home.

While Nora crushed herbs in a small wooden dish with a knife handle, Sean carefully removed the shirt strips and moss from Úna's arm. To my great relief the bleeding had stopped.

"You were always a terror for cuts and bruises," Lee observed, placing the crushed herbs on the open wound and tying them in place with a strip of clean linen. "Do you remember the time you fell off your father's horse? You couldn't have been more than four or five. And the time you tried to swim out to the castle and Seamus the Herd had to swim out after you?"

"I would have reached it if he hadn't stopped me," Úna protested.

"Oh, would you now?" Lee grinned. "Then there was the time you borrowed my currach and rowed it onto the rock. I tell you," he looked at me, "this girl has more lives than a cat."

"What about the times my brothers nearly killed themselves?" Úna said. "Nobody talks about them." Despite her protest, I could see she was pleased with the recital of her youthful mishaps.

"You were all a bit wild," Sean conceded, "but – and I'm telling no lie – you were the worst. And you haven't changed – fighting with skeans! Whoever heard of such antics? And from a girl!"

"Will you give me *gafann* to help me sleep?" Úna asked.

"Will I what?" Sean exclaimed, "And have Cathal Roe down here in the morning! No, I'll give you more *slanus* to spread on the cut and something to drink that will help with the healing."

Nora now begged us to have a piece of griddlecake and a *meadar* of ale but I demurred, reminding Úna that her family would be expecting us.

"You go back," she began to stroke the cat, "I'm staying here."

Since she seemed so adamant, I reluctantly bade goodbye to Sean and Nora, then with a heavy heart set out for the mansion. What would Turlough think of somebody who had wounded his sister with a skean?

ಬ

Chapter 10

There was dismay in the Great Hall when I related what had happened. Charles Roe began to question me angrily until Turlough raised an admonitory hand. From the glances they exchanged I deduced that each knew in his heart I wasn't to blame. When Lady Margaret urged Turlough to hurry down to Lee's cabin I gave it as my opinion that Úna wouldn't return.

"Listen," Turlouogh made a sudden decision, "why don't you keep Daibhí here for a few days while he gathers information for the Annals? Úna, Eamonn and I will ride back to Cloonybrien."

The family agreed to this request with the result that it was decided I would be sharing Niall's cabin. In the meantime Lady Margaret showed me about the library, which was at the west end of the house. Having never seen any printed book but that used by the priest at mass, the rows of leather-bound volumes packed side by side on shelves amazed me. Flanking them was a tapestry showing the Death of Adonis and a picture of the Children of Lir being turned into swans by their stepmother Aoife.

"Who painted that?" I asked in admiration.

"Oh, it was done by Úna," Lady Margaret said. "I much prefer that portrait she did of herself." She indicated a picture of Úna as a girl of about fifteen hanging above a desk on which a pair of eyeglasses, called spectacles, rested.

"Those were my husband's," Lady Margaret explained. "He used to sit at that desk reading and copying passages from his books. Look," she showed me a sheet of paper. "That was the last thing he wrote before he set out for Athlone. It was about his father, Brian. Úna was always on at him about how heroic his father was and he would point out that Brian had twice attacked Boyle Abbey and that together with other Connacht chiefs he had surrendered his lands to the Crown so that afterwards he might hold them by English law. 'But he fought to make himself chief,' Úna would object, and the argument would rage on. She was always teasing that his years in Trinity had turned him into an Englishman and he would remind her that Brian had married twice under Brehon law but that that hadn't prevented him from marrying Maeve O'Conor Sligo so that their children would be legitimate under English law – you saw Maeve's portrait outside on the wall. I'm only telling you this because you'll learn it for yourself when you read through the Annals."

Maybe Lady Margaret truly believed that that was why she spoke so frankly but over the years I've discovered that once people learn I'm a scribe they are eager to confide in me – Perhaps by doing so they hope that it's their view of things which will be written down? As for those she termed "ragamuffins", they look on penmanship as a form of magic, which, in a way, it is.

"By the way, Úna didn't really get you to fight her with a skean, did she?" Lady Margaret continued.

"Why do you ask that?" I put on a surprised expression.

"Because I know my daughter," she replied. "It's not the first time she tried to harm herself. Did she tell you about the time she swallowed *gafann*?"

I shook my head. "If we hadn't got Sir Robert's physician to come out from Abbeyboyle I don't believe she'd have pulled through. That was because her father wouldn't let her out to see Costello. If I tell you these things it's because you're our scribe and Turlough says we can be frank with you."

Before giving me the Annals, she showed me the charter of King James, granting the manor castle and demesne to her husband, which, she emphasised, was only a fraction of what his father Brian had owned. It was written in ornate characters on massive sheets, and though it was in Latin I could make nearly everything out.

"That was given to my husband less than twenty years ago," she explained, "and then that horrible Wentworth began to question our title to the very lands set down in it. Poor Brian! I knew something awful was going to happen the morning he set out for Athlone." Tears began to trickle down her cheek, and leaving me to peruse the Annals, she hurried from the library.

As I sat at the desk carefully turning the handwritten pages, I was aware that my kinsmen had transcribed them for Úna's grandfather, though Brian had made some of the entries himself: one for A.D.1581 expressed his desolation after the death of Calvach O'Conor Sligo, his wife's brother. It was, he states, written by him in *Carraig-Mic-Diarmada*, his castle on the rock. On examining the sheet left by Úna's father before he set out for Athlone, I saw that it concerned his half brothers, Rory and Tadhg. They had claimed a right to Moylurg lands under Brehon law – So Brian Oge was under attack from his own people as well as from the foreigners!

At this point, I looked up and my eyes met Úna's, gazing at me from the portrait. How often must her father, dispirited from reading and writing about past glories and lost opportunities, have looked at that tender, wistful face? Then another question occurred to me: did Lady Margaret ever feel that her own portrait, not her daughter's, should have hung there?

Brushing this thought aside, I returned to the Annals. Under the year A.D. 1540 I saw where Úna's great-grandfather Rory and his wife Sadhbh Burke gave a feast on The Rock to which, among others, the poets and ollaves of Erin were invited. Wine flowed and rich gifts were distributed in "the Oxford of hospitality and wisdom of the province of Connacht." As I read about this feast I couldn't help wondering if there were any O'Duigenans present. Then I turned to the entry for A.D.1549 when Rory was elected King of Moylurg. On this occasion he had again invited the learned men of Erin to a great feast but what caught my eye was a foray he conducted in the same year against the Costellos in which three score cows were taken and given to the poets and ollaves – So Thomas's ancestors hadn't done all the raiding! Rory had also been Abbot of Trinity Island in Lough Key. Under the year A.D.1568 his death was recorded and it was clear from the entry that he was considered the greatest ruler the

MacDermots ever had and that after him came the ruin and destruction of their power.

That evening as we were sitting on *súgán* chairs before the cabin fire I asked Niall about Thomas. While he filled a short-stemmed clay pipe with tobacco he told me that, like the Burkes and the Dillons, the Costellos had been Old Gall. Years previously they had taken the territory in Mayo now known as the Barony of Costello-Gallen from the O'Garas.

"Of course..." He touched a glowing ember to his pipe, meanwhile puffing rapidly. "Of course that was the way of things back then. What's that saying, the one about getting land through the sword?"

" 'The land of Ireland is sword-land,'" I recited the line from O'Huiginn's famous poem.

"That's it!" he cried. "Sword-land. Anyway, the Costellos were now living cheek by jowl with the MacDermots so the two families fought tooth and nail, especially in the time of Rory, Úna's great-grandfather. Today the Dillons own Costello-Gallen and Thomas's people are just tenants. I can tell you that rankled with Jordan Boy, Thomas's father. "

"Tell me," I leaned forward eagerly, "is it true that Jordan Boy was a great poet?"

"A great poet is it?" Niall removed the pipe from his mouth and blew out smoke. "Well now, Úna's father, God rest his soul, used to refer to him as a 'street poet' – it seems he didn't compose in the proper bardic style. Úna maintains that Thomas himself is great at composing, but I'll leave it to scholars like yourself to be the judge of that."

"Where does Thomas live?" I asked.

"In Tullaghanmore, beyond Lough Techet." He put more tobacco into his pipe. "It's northwest of Dungar, where the family of Rory MacDermot, Brian Oge's half brother, lives – Rory himself died four years ago. Lord have mercy on them both."

"So Thomas would have to ride all that distance just to see Úna?" I observed.

"Oh, that'd be nothing to the same man," Niall smiled. "Sure he'd sleep out under the stars if he had to – A wild Mayo *spalpaire* Brian Oge used to call him. Still, if he couldn't ride back to Tullaghanmore because of darkness or bad weather it's likely he could stay with friends of his below in Ardcarn."

"I saw him before mass today," I said. "Does he come to Kilbryan every Sunday?"

"You'll have to ask Úna that." Niall gave me an amused glance. "You're not thinking of waylaying him?"

"Why?" I asked. "Is he dangerous?"

"He killed a wrestler in Sligo," Niall spat into the fire, "and they say he could flatten an ox with one blow of his fist. Still, if Úna loves him he can't be just a *spalpaire* – maybe she reckons he's like her grandfather, a warrior and a scholar?"

"I was told she met him when she was staying in Bellanagare," I continued. "Is Bellanagare far from here?"

"About a good half-day's ride," he said. "You should ask Úna to take you there the next time they let her visit Eleanor's sister."

ଔ

Chapter 11

Apart from worry about Úna, the next few days in Carrick Mansion passed pleasantly. I spent much of that time in the library studying the Annals and looking through books such as *England's Helicon* and *The Shepheardes Calendar,* but having difficulty reading English, could only marvel at the abundance of neatly printed words stored between the covers. Was it, I asked myself, this proof of English learning which had kept Brian Oge from throwing in his lot with O'Neill and O'Donnell in the last war? When I put the question to Niall he pointed out that Brian Oge was only about eleven when fighting broke out, though he would have been sixteen at the time of the Curlew Pass: his cousin, Conor Oge, who had played a leading part in that victory, had been made chief in his place by Red Hugh O'Donnell.

Since I now realised that in order to complete the Annals I would have to find out more about Úna's father, I decided to discuss him with Honora, who next day wandered into the library. Pulling her shawl tighter, even though the day was warm, she told me that while Brian Oge had devoted little time to her education or Margaret's, he would spend hours teaching Úna in that very room. She was the apple of his eye, no matter how often she disobeyed him or got into trouble. She then recounted various youthful escapades, some of which Sean Lee had mentioned.

"When did she first try to harm herself?" I asked.

"Oh, that would have been after Margaret's wedding." She sat on the chair I offered her. "Margaret married Conn, the son of Brian Oge O'Rourke of Breifne."

"Brian Oge of the Battle Axes?" I drew up my stool beside her.

She nodded. "Anyway, father said that it was now Úna's turn to give us a wedding and he had just the man in mind for her".

" 'Who would that be?' she asked.

" 'Hugh O'Conor of Ballintober, O'Conor Don's heir,' he told her.

45

" 'You're just trying to get rid of me,' she accused.

" 'No, I'm not: I thought you'd be delighted,' he said. 'As you know, he's a direct descendant of the kings of Connacht and the last High King of Ireland.'

"Úna didn't say another word but the next day she wouldn't talk or leave her bed. She refused to get up or eat for three whole days. Then Eleanor suggested sending her to Bellanagare Castle to be a companion for Anne and that brought her out of her sulk. The only trouble was that she met Thomas in Bellanagare."

I sensed that jealousy of her sister was making her eager to confide in me, so I remarked, "Úna told me that your father wanted her to marry Sir Robert King's son."

"That was after Hugh got betrothed to Isabel Burke," she explained. "When Úna eventually met Hugh she realised what a fool she'd been – He's really handsome and daring. Anyway, father decided next that John King would make a good husband but by that time Úna had her heart set on Costello – He's a poet and they say he's fearless but his people are only tenants of the Dillons."

"Something just occurred to me." I picked up Brian Oge's hand-written sheet. "Did your father leave any other writings apart from this?"

"You'll have to ask mother that." She studied me with her pale blue eyes as she rose from her chair. "He was always writing about the history of our family – as if that would somehow make up for everything we've lost or are about to lose."

When Honora had returned to the Great Hall, I decided to write a rough outline of Brian Oge's obituary in order to have something to show Turlough. Copying the style of the Annals, I began in the following manner:

The kalends of January on Sunday; A.D.1636

Brian Oge, son of Brian, son of Rory, son of Teige, son of Rory Oge, i.e. lord of Moylurg, and Airtech, and Tir-Tuathail, the best man of his age, and estate, and high lordship, that came of the Gael of the West of Europe in his own time...

I was tempted to give his lineage back to Conn of the Hundred Battles or at least to Dermot, the 12th century king of Moylurg from whom the family derived its name, but thought better of it. Recalling the line about minstrels in O'Mulconry's elegy, I praised Brian Oge for his generosity to them, after first mentioning his patronage of ollaves, poets and men of learning, his assistance to maidens, innocents and orphans and his loyalty to the True Church and men of God. Since there was so much, however, that I had yet to learn about this man who had lived in the Gaelic world of Connacht as well as the New Gall world of Dublin, I decided to talk to Lady Margaret before proceeding any further.

She answered my first questions readily enough, telling me how Brian Oge, his brothers and sisters had, after the death of their father, gone to live with their mother's people, the O'Conors Sligo; how in 1604, three years after the defeat of O'Neill and O'Donnell at Kinsale, he had been made a ward of court – The wardship was granted to Sir Theobald Dillon, at which time he, Brian Oge, was studying in Trinity, where the Queen's ministers had sent him with the intention of turning him into a loyal subject. In this aim, however, they had failed as her husband had never turned his back on his own people or abandoned the True Faith.

At this point I asked if Brian Oge had left any writings apart from the single sheet on the library desk. Immediately her demeanour changed. If he had written other things, they were of a private nature. What should concern me was his goodness to his people and his efforts to shield them from the hot words of idle tongues. It was easy to preach rebellion, but he understood that a tree that didn't bend with the wind would be blown down. There had always been too much fighting in Ireland and not enough thinking.

That very evening Cathal Roe, who spent much of each day outdoors inspecting herds and flocks or directing his workers, suggested that if I went back to Cloonybrien I might be able to persuade Úna to return home – It occurred to me that my departure would also keep me from asking his mother impolitic questions! So it was that after filling a saddlebag with a sheaf of writing paper, a horn of ink and half a dozen goose quills, I rode away on Banbawn and was entering Turlough's house before nightfall.

Úna seemed pleased to see me. Her arm was almost healed and as soon as I had eaten, she insisted on walking with me to the cabin. On the way, she confided that Turlough had told her that the shrine of the Virgin in Trinity Island was in danger of being broken. It seemed that Cathal Roe had learned from Sir Robert King that the Cootes considered it an abomination and that if Sir Robert didn't destroy it there were those that would. Now the shrine was carved from stone and set in the abbey wall, facing the altar. If she and I, together with Thomas and his servant, would row over to the island one night we cold remove the shrine and carry it off to the castle.

"What if Sir Robert catches us?" I objected.

"He wants us to save it," she assured me. "Why do you think he told Cathal Roe? Trinity Island belongs to him, so while he may not like our people going there to visit the shrine, he doesn't want it smashed either."

"Is this shrine very old?" I asked.

"Yes," she replied. "Father told us that before the King of Moylurg set out to seek help from Robert the Bruce to expel the English, he first prayed at the shrine. Maybe that's why the Cootes want to destroy it: they're afraid it'll give us courage."

I was about to point out that, according to the Annals, the Connacht chiefs had not supported Edward, Robert the Bruce's brother, when he landed in Ireland but decided to keep quiet. While her plan seemed foolish, Úna's thoughts flashed like lightning, illuminating everything around in an instant and, though sometimes I was loath to admit it, in countless ways her learning surpassed my own. She had her father to thank for that. He had taught her to read and write, something my own mother and sisters couldn't do, and he had passed on to her much of the knowledge he had acquired in Trinity College. Perhaps in my inmost mind I believed that if I yoked my endeavours to hers together they would be far more fruitful. At all events, I hadn't the heart to oppose something which had plainly restored her spirits, and so it was that she led me willy-nilly into my first dangerous adventure.

CB

Chapter 12

It was dark on Trinity Island, the light from the pine torch Thomas held aloft throwing a lurid, uncertain glare on the wall of the roofless church. He and Úna led the way, and Peadar, his servant, Manus, a burly Ulsterman, and I followed, picking our way past jutting tree branches, fallen gravestones and low mounds with wooden crosses. Here many of Úna's ancestors were buried, among them the great Rory, who had been both king and abbot. Somewhere nearby was also the grave of Clifford, the English Governor of Connacht, whose headless body had been buried by Conor Oge MacDermot after the Battle of the Curlews. Behind us our two currachs were resting on the rocky shore, where we had carried them after rowing across the lough from Cloontykilla to avoid been seen by people in the village.

When we finally entered the church the arched window openings showed that it had been more ornate than Kilbryan but what caught the eye was the shrine fixed in the left wall, facing the altar. This was an oblong stone, a little over two feet high and one foot broad. On it was carved the Virgin seated on a throne with the child Jesus on her lap. The Virgin was wearing a crown and the child had rays coming from his head. Under the shrine were two recesses with pointed arches, flanked by small columns topped by carved skulls. A pile of skulls and bones was left in each recess so that my mind filled with horror as if the dead were watching us.

"I'll have to stand on your shoulders, Manus, to get at the top." Thomas's words brought me back to reality.

"No," Úna interjected. "Let me try. I'm lighter."

I offered to make the first attempt but Úna wouldn't be dissuaded.

Thomas gave me the torch then helped Úna onto Manus's shoulders, holding her ankles to prevent her from falling. Peadar handed her a small bar he was carrying and soon the night rang with the clang of iron as Úna chipped at the wall surrounding the shrine. While the stones were being prized out and tossed to the ground I couldn't help feeling that sooner or later we would all be punished for this desecration. As if to confirm my foreboding a fragment struck Peadar's head.

"Cross of Christ!" he shouted. "Do you want to kill me?"

"Quiet!" Thomas commanded. "Why don't you go out and see if any boat is heading this way? And bring back two oars!"

Peadar set off, grumbling indignantly, "How am I supposed to find my way in the dark? Am I an owl?"

"If you're not an owl, don't screech like one," Thomas called out.

After what seemed an eternity Úna tired and I took her place, standing on Thomas's shoulders to give Manus a rest. It was difficult keeping my balance and wielding the iron bar in the fitful light of the torch, which Úna now held. Soon, however, there were only a few stones holding the shrine in position. Thomas let me descend then he got Manus to support him while he wrenched at the shrine. Úna was holding the torch and I was holding Thomas's shins and keeping my head bowed to stop mortar falling into my eyes when, suddenly, Manus began to give way.

"Where are the blasted oars?" he groaned.

"Hold on!" Thomas encouraged. "Daibhí, tell that fool Peadar to hurry!"

I rushed out and stumbled towards the currachs, meeting Peadar on the path.

"Quick!" I cried, grabbing an oar. "What kept you?"

"There's a boat out on the lough," he said. "I was on my way back this minute to warn ye."

"Prop it up with the oars!" Thomas yelled when we entered.

Peadar and I each got an oar under the shrine but by this time Manus could hold on no longer. As in a nightmare I saw Thomas let go of the carved edge before he and Manus toppled to the ground. For a minute it seemed that the oars would keep the shrine up but a slight shift in one of them caused it to unbalance.

Next moment it was falling. I'll never forget the clatter with which it struck the floor, the noise filling the church like a clap of doom. However, by some miracle, the oars were lying under it and only one corner with a carved dove broke off.

The nightmare was still not over because we had to extinguish our torch for fear those approaching the island would notice the light – that is if they hadn't seen it already. Luckily, apart from some cuts and bruises, none of us was badly injured. Úna and I crept down the path but though we looked in all directions we could see no sign of a boat. When we told Thomas he was furious with Peadar but Úna reminded him that it wasn't Peadar's fault if he thought he saw something and, anyway, we were less likely to be detected if we worked in the dark.

After much fumbling about, Thomas and Manus carried the shrine out, with Úna leading the way, and Peadar and I bringing up the rear. I had both arms about the carved dove, determined to save it should I trip and fall. By the time we were afloat once more my head was aching with the strain. Thomas, Úna and Peadar had the shrine in their currach, and Manus and I were rowing after them in the second one when Manus spotted a light rounding the north corner of Trinity Island. Putting on a spurt, we caught up with the others.

"*Fainic!*" Manus shouted but they too had seen the moving light.

Rowing like demons we headed for MacDermot's Rock, knowing that once in the castle we would be safe. Whoever was following clung to our wake like a will-o'-the-wisp, bobbing and weaving behind us. Presently another light flared; there was a dull report and something struck the water ahead.

"Was that a musket?" I asked, having never been fired at before.

"Aye," Manus said. "If you were living in Ulster you'd ken the sound well enough. The Planters there would as soon shoot a Papist as a wolf."

Hoping that a moving boat would make it difficult to reload and prime a musket, we redoubled our efforts, arms

53

flailing, so that the massive walls of the castle were soon looming against the night sky. Manus and I continued to row frantically, rounding the Rock alongside the other currach. To our relief, the boat did not follow, its light veering off northward.

We slowed down as we approached the castle, whose outer wall rose steeply from the water's edge. At one point there was a recess with stone steps leading up to a narrow entrance. In no time we were ashore and while we tied up the currachs, Úna mounted the steps and pulled on a bell rope hanging beside an iron door. Every moment we expected the boat to swing back but it didn't: either our attackers feared being fired on from the castle or they were content to have chased us away from Trinity Island. Soon the bobbing light faded away to the northeast. Since Arigna lay in that direction it strengthened our suspicion that the Cootes or their minions were behind the attack.

After repeated ringing of the bell, an old porter with a lantern arrived to open the door. Grumbling that it was an outrageous hour to rouse him, he led us down a passageway, through the bawn and inside the castle. Here in a small, barrel-vaulted room Father Bernard was pulling on his habit by the light of a candle. He had just risen from his pallet, which with a table, chair and an oaken chest comprised the furniture. On learning that we had carried off the shrine, he was overjoyed until Thomas and Manus brought it in.

"Oh, no!" he cried. "God save us all, if the White Canons saw it like this! Still, the way times are changing, you couldn't have left it there."

When Úna promised that Rory would fit the corner so neatly in place, people wouldn't even know it had been broken, Father Bernard's face brightened.

"Look at me lamenting over a shrine," he said, " and our own beautiful abbey roofless and its chapel used for Lutheran services. I'm like Oisín after the Fenians, the only Cistercian left in Moylurg. Still, Sir Robert isn't a bad man – though I can't say the same for those Cootes. We'll get Rory to fix the shrine into the oratory wall; then our people can come here to ask Mary to intercede for them with her Divine Son. Yes, great blessings will flow from your work this night – I'm sure of it."

Despite Father Bernard's words my forebodings persisted.

CB

Chapter 13

The sun was rising by the time Úna and I set off on our horses for Cloonybrien. Luckily, Turlough would still be absent, having ridden to Dunamon Castle with Eamonn earlier in the week to see his wife. Úna hadn't told him of her plan to take the shrine from Trinity Island, not knowing if he would approve. We were, therefore, sharing another secret, a realisation that made me uneasy since Turlough was my master.

"We should have got his permission," I reminded her.

"No," she replied. "If somebody accuses him of being behind last night's work, he can swear with a clear conscience that he wasn't. I know he would have liked to come with us but as chieftain his hands are tied."

"And would he have approved of your two helpers, Thomas and Manus?" I was curious to see how she would reply.

"Why shouldn't he?" she asked in surprise. "Anyway, he knows I've seen him with Eithne and Siobhan – Not that I'd ever tell Mairéad. Turlough and Teige are the only ones in our family that didn't turn against me."

"He didn't agree then with your father's choice of suitors?" I remarked.

"Why are you asking all these questions?" she demanded. "I suppose little Honora has been filling your head with lies about me."

"She told me about John King and Hugh O'Conor," I admitted. "That was because I was trying to understand your father's attitude in order to write his obituary, the one I showed you."

"Oh yes," she scoffed, "the one about the noble, generous scholar who helped maidens and orphans!"

Fearful of turning her thoughts in on herself once more, I pointed out that the obituary was just something to let Turlough see that I hadn't been wasting my time. She and he could finish it in whatever way they pleased.

"You must think me an ungrateful child." Her voice was barely audible. "And I suppose I am. It's just that we could almost understand each other without speech. I was his muse. Yes, that's what he called me once: Euterpe, the muse who inspires music and poetry."

"I never heard of her." I was anxious to keep her talking. "We were told in Castlefore that it was the goddess Brigid who inspired poets."

She didn't answer, her eyes fixed on the way ahead, and it was in this silent manner we finished our journey.

After breakfast I threw myself on my pallet in the cabin and felt as if I had just fallen asleep when Eithne roused me. My brother Philip was after arriving, his garron lathered with sweat. When I made my way to the house, Philip rose from the table.

"It's father," he blurted out. "He's dying."

On questioning him I learned that father had collapsed while digging a drain in the bog. The healer who examined him believed he wouldn't last another day – so my forebodings were coming true. That very evening we set out for home on two fresh garrons Rory provided, explaining that I could bring both back whenever I returned.

After that life took on the nature of a dream in which everything happens just beyond ones control. Even before we rode in the boreen to our cottage, the keening told us we were too late. My married sister Noreen, who lived nearby, came out to whisper that father had died soon after Philip left. I remember handing her the gold sovereigns Turlough had given me for my poem to pay for the funeral then I was shaking hands with relatives and neighbours before embracing my mother and Eileen and kneeling by the table on which father was laid out with pennies resting on his eyes, his face turned to bleached stone.

For the rest of that day and the succeeding night I sat around almost numb, listening to the keening women praise my father's generosity or the old men, as they smoked long clay pipes or drank meaders of ale, recount his youthful exploits during the war, when he had taken part in the siege of Collooney Castle, which O'Conor Sligo was holding for the Queen. If only I had spoken to him of those times when he was alive... Better still, if only I had given him the gold sovereigns to repay the sacrifices he and my mother had made so that I could study in Castlefore...

I got a few hours sleep before the priest, Father Malachy, arrived late next morning. When I was a young mass server Father Malachy, out of kindness, had begun to teach me Latin in his home, using hand-written passages from the great Roman writers, Caesar, Virgil and Cicero. Now I mumbled the Latin responses as he said the prayers for the dead. After that, father's body was put into a newlymade deal coffin, which was placed on our farm cart, and with screeching and lamentation we set out for the graveyard. There was a great crowd of our neighbours standing around the open grave but imagine my surprise when I spied Úna and Rory among them.

When the burial was over Úna came up to shake hands with me, then with mother, Eileen, Philip and Noreen. It was clear that everyone was marvelling that such a beautiful and strangely dressed young woman should have taken the trouble to attend a scullogue's funeral. Even Father Malachy was beaming like a small boy when he greeted her. Of course he knew all about the MacDermots and asked after them and Father Bernard. He, Úna and Rory accompanied us back to the house, much to my unease, for I didn't want Úna to see the small, two-room cottage in which we lived.

If Úna was struck by our humble conditions she gave no sign of it. Indeed the pleasure she took in the dinner Noreen prepared was touching. It was as if she had never tasted such well-cooked food before. After the meal, while mother went outside with Eileen to talk to neighbours and Philip and Rory discussed crops and cattle, Father Malachy chatted to Úna and me about the siege of Collooney Castle, which, he maintained, had ended when Clifford's head was tossed over the battlements. Úna quickly pointed out that it was Brian Oge O'Rourke and not her kinsman, Brian Oge MacDermot, who had ordered the beheading

59

of the English general after he was slain in the Battle of the Curlews.

"And O'Rourke was an Oxford student," I couldn't help adding.

"It just goes to show what terrible things men do when they resort to arms," Father Malachy observed. "As the Romans put it, *Homo homini lupus*: man is a wolf to man. May God grant you young people never see war in your lifetime."

"Isn't living like slaves worst than war?" Úna said, and the two of them got into a heated dispute about the rights and wrongs of fighting for ones land now that Wentworth was about to plant Connacht.

"It's not Wentworth we need fear so much as the Puritans," Father Malachy declared. "They keep on badgering His Majesty to stop the Lutheran ministers beyond in England from preaching so-called 'Catholic' doctrines. If they and their ilk ever get the upper hand here, we'll think the present troubles nothing."

This led to a discussion of the Cootes, in particular of Old Sir Charles, who, Father Malachy reminded us, had fought against the Irish at Kinsale and was now not only a great landowner but also vice-president of Connacht. When Father Malachy heard about how we had been fired on as we brought the shrine from Trinity Island he warned us not to reveal to another living soul what we had done lest word get back to Castlecoote.

"You may not be so lucky the next time," he warned us.

This observation was borne in on me a week later when Rory arrived with a letter from Úna telling me that the Cootes were harrying Sir Robert about the removal of the shrine. She had been obliged to reveal my part in it, and to show that he didn't condone what had taken place, Turlough had told Sir Robert that he was dismissing me from his service. It would be better therefore if I didn't return to Cloonybrien till the whole matter had blown over. She was enclosing a letter, which Turlough had written to Tadhg Oge O'Flaherty of Red Island in Lough Mask recommending me as a tutor or chronicler. In addition, Rory had fifteen shillings to give me, which together with one of the garrons should get me safely to Tadhg Oge's castle.

So it was that my exile began, an exile that was to last five long years. Were it not for the letters Úna sent me I would never have stayed in Galway.

⁋

Chapter 14

If the MacDermots were hospitable the O'Flaherty's – who kept the old Gaelic way of life – were every bit their equal, so that, when not teaching their young sons History or Irish writing, I was allowed to continue my work on *The Pursuit of Diarmuid and Grainne*. Nevertheless, night and morning I missed Úna and worried that she might again harm herself if I weren't at hand to prevent it.

It was now that I began to see the similarity between her and Grainne. Both were strong-willed girls, who would not accept suitors their fathers had chosen for them. When the High King, Cormac Mac Art, wanted Grainne to marry the ageing Finn Mac Cumhail, she first tried her wiles on his son Oisin then decided that Diarmuid was the only man she could love. Diarmuid, however, refused to flee with someone promised to his Fenian chief until she put a *geis* on him.

Of course there's another way of looking at this, as an old Mayo storyteller reminded me. She pointed out that Diarmuid had a love spot on his forehead and any woman who saw it couldn't help loving him. If that were so then Grainne wasn't really to blame for persuading him to elope with her. Maybe Thomas hadn't a love spot, but like Diarmuid he was a warrior who was beloved of women. Anyway, he could hardly have failed to be captivated by Úna once she had decided he was the one she wanted. But in the heel of the hunt did she only want him to thwart her father? Was her sister Honora right when she suggested that Úna could have loved Hugh O'Conor just as well, had she met him in time?

Perhaps in my inmost heart I knew I was clutching at straws but it helped me to imagine that at some point of crisis Úna might still be won by someone who, though no warrior, admired her intelligence and ardent spirit. Not that I was likely to be at hand if such a crisis should arise. This was borne in on me as month after month dragged by without any word from Cloonybrien. I had almost given up hope when one day in late autumn a piper named Kevin arrived at the castle. Kevin, a small, middle-aged man with mischievous twinkling eyes, made his living by wandering round Connacht asking for hospitality at noble houses and since he carried letters and tales from one place to another this was seldom refused. The O'Flahertys had their own harper but the lively dance tunes Kevin played were popular with the entire household, especially the younger servants.

After supper in the Great Hall the very first evening, Kevin whispered that he had something for me. When I questioned him later in his room, he gave me an expectant glance. "Did you never hear what the thrush sang to the young scholar?" He grinned before answering his own question: "'Spend away; spend away; God will send your way' – or, to put the matter plainly, 'Money will make the mare go.'"

"You're talking in riddles," I pretended not to understand.

"That's because you have wax in your ears," he chuckled. "Tell me this, scribe, can you wag one ear without moving the other?"

"No," I admitted, whereupon he wagged one of his own ears with his hand.

"Any fool could do that," I pointed out.

"Then why didn't you do it?" he crowed.

"You're a joker," I told him. "Have you something for me or not?"

"Patience, scribe!" he wagged his finger. "That's no way to talk to someone who brings tidings from a beautiful maiden."

"What tidings?" My heart gave a joyful leap as he extracted a small packet from his satchel. "Here!" I offered him a shilling.

"Now I know why Jesus warned people to beware of the scribes." He stared at the coin in his palm as if he couldn't see it.

"What have you got against scribes?" I protested, knowing well Úna would have paid him already.

"Nothing," he admitted, "except that while a scholar like yourself lives here at his ease I have to wander from castle to castle and village to godforsaken village in wind and cold and wet. Then when I bring you this...this likely declaration of love, which I've carried safely all the way from Moylurg, you offer me a mite."

Begging his forgiveness, I gave him another shilling, at which he handed me the packet, saying that Úna had commanded that once I had read the letter inside, I was to burn it in his presence.

"Why did she say that?" I asked, examining the packet's tightly knotted cord.

"Ah, she's a strange one," he rubbed his chin, "beautiful but headstrong. A girl like that needs careful handling. It's not a scribe but a warrior she should wed. You'll be hard put to rein her in."

On cutting the cord with my skean, I drew out a letter sealed in numerous places with sealing wax. By the light of a candle I eagerly began to read:

To my true friend and comrade, Daibhí

It is now almost a month since you left us and knowing that you were obliged to depart hurriedly after removing the shrine, I'm going to tell you about everything which has happened since. I have been living in Croghan with the O'Mulloys because Turlough was displeased with me over the raid on Trinity Island and life in Carrick Mansion is unbearable. It is much more pleasant here because Teige is with me and we can go riding to Lisadaly and Canbo loughs, where there is a castle that once belonged to us and later to the O'Mulloys but is now in the possession of the Lamberts from Yorkshire.

Josias Lambert invited us in for dinner; Teige wanted to accept but I was afraid he might be hoping to get information from us that he could pass on to the Cootes. It's very hard to know whom you can trust. Josias's wife, Anne, is the daughter of John Crofton, who got Canbo at the time of The Composition of Connacht. If father were alive he could explain the ins and outs of how this castle changed hands so many times. What matters is that what was once a part of our patrimony is now in the hands of the New Gall.

Teige is a year younger than me, and still unmarried, so we get along well together. He would love to go overseas to be with our brother Bryan, who is a captain in the Spanish Netherlands – I am only telling you about Bryan because I know I can trust you. If the family ever found out that I told you they would kill me. That's why you must burn this letter as soon as you've read it. I have instructed Kevin that he makes sure you do this. It's impossible to know who will pass on information – I told you that I suspect Eamonn, though Turlough doesn't agree with me. If the likes of the Cootes ever found out that Bryan was fighting for the Spaniards they would use it against us. I'll explain more about Bryan when we next meet.

Mother wanted me to stay with her family in Derrymaclachny, which is in Galway County. I know she wishes to keep me as far away from Thomas as possible. God forbid that a child of hers should marry a mere Costello – After all, her mother's father was Earl of Clanrickard! She forgets that the same man was known as 'Richard the Sassenach' and her uncle, Lord Dunkellin, who became the third Earl, fought with the English at the Curlew Pass and Kinsale. How father could have married such a woman I'll never understand. Now here's a secret: if Teige can borrow enough money he'll take me with him to the Spanish Netherlands. Won't that be wonderful? I'll soon be twenty-two years of age, so I don't see why I shouldn't go overseas like my brothers. If Teige reneges, I'll get Thomas to take me.

Father Bernard got Rory to set up the shrine in the castle oratory as he said he would. The oratory is on the upper floor, behind the Great Hall. I went there before I set out for Croghan and in the candlelight Mary and Jesus look almost alive. Father Malachy asked me to paint the Annunciation on a wooden panel, which he will place at the left of the shrine – he has one of a white canon, which will stand at the other side. I'm painting Mary at present and telling her that if she helps me to do it right I'll serve her like a nun. Everybody here thinks my picture is beautiful. Even Teige says he likes it, so I'm going to make Gabriel look like him!

I must finish this letter quickly, as Kevin will soon be leaving Croghan on his way to Dungar, where he will stay with our cousins before travelling to Ballyhaunis and the West. When Father took me with him to Galway City we used to stop one or two nights in Derrymaclachny Castle. Those were happy days, now gone forever.

Wishing you happiness with the O'Flahertys and good success with your work on the Story of Diarmuid and Grainne, I commit you to the protection of Mary. From my room in Croghan, the 2 of June, 1636. Úna.

In keeping with Úna's request I burned the letter, which I am setting down here from memory. I wish I could have saved everything she wrote as you would then know by her own hand what a strange girl she was, planning to fight for the Spaniards one minute, talking of being a nun the next. That she was a true artist I confirmed when I eventually saw her painting of the Annunciation with its serene Virgin and bright-winged angel. That she could sing like a lark I already knew. And, yet, her anger at her parents was not what my own sisters would have understood or approved. There was a hurt in her whose roots went deep into the past, maybe even beyond the time when the portrait hanging above her father's desk was painted.

Before Kevin left again on his travels I paid him to deliver two letters, one written to Úna, the other to my mother – whose name was also Úna – telling both that I hoped to be home by the following spring. In truth, I was feeling guilty as well as homesick for I knew my family could have used my help now that father was no longer with them. Did Úna I wondered, for all her accusations, miss her father even more than I missed mine?

❧

Chapter 15

If I had realised back then what terrible evils were to befall our country I would not have been so eager to wish my sojourn on Lough Mask over. Through the five years I lived with the O'Flahertys, stories reached us of Catholics fighting Protestants in Europe, of trouble brewing between Charles and his parliament in England and the Scots turning against their king, but these were like thunder rumbling over the Partry mountains, threatening a storm that didn't come nearer. Of course there were bad signs at home as well: shortages of grain as harvests failed; the spectre of plantation hanging over Connacht; New Gall such as the Cootes and their ilk stealthily acquiring land and power at the expense of our people, but on the face of it there were no great changes in fortune.

As for me I had got myself entangled with one of the kitchen maids, a warm-hearted girl who, probably because she was unlettered herself, looked on me as a kind of prince. Our daillance caused me much unease, knowing that were she to consider us betrothed, her brothers and father would compel me to marry her. Whenever I attempted to withdraw from this entanglement she sought me out and, like a man with a craving for usquebagh, I yielded recklessly to her kisses. Afterwards I would curse myself for having betrayed the highborn girl to whom I had given my heart.

Now and then a letter from Úna arrived, a gift of fairy gold that quickly turned to dust because she always gave instructions that I was to burn her letters once I had read them – Though my memory is good, it would have consoled me when downcast to feast my eyes on the twining, back-sloping characters in which she had set out her thoughts. There was one other thing that rankled: she made no mention of a time being set for my return. Could it be that Turlough had decided never to summon me back to Cloonybrien? Was Úna content that I should remain a distant friend to whom she could write in times of loneliness?

One letter that Kevin brought near the end of my exile will serve
to show how she was changing in my absence:

To my true friend, Daibhí

Everything is going wrong since I last wrote to you. I'm
back again in this prison, with nobody to talk to except Bridgeen
and Eleanor – I don't say anything to Honora because she would
tell mother, and Brian and Terence are too young to understand.
Thomas has found service with Hugh Oge O'Conor in Castlerea
– his brother Dudley is with O'Conor Don in Ballintober. I
wanted to visit Castlerea but my tyrant of a brother, Cathal Roe,
wouldn't allow it. "You'll not shame us by going where you
weren't invited," he said. Of course mother supported him, so I
refused to eat anything for a week. When Turlough told Thomas
he rode all the way from Castlerea to see me.

Turlough doesn't come here much, probably because he
owes Cathal Roe money – he recently sold eight quarters of land
to Sir Charles Coote – and Teige, instead of taking me overseas
as he promised, has become chief steward for the O'Mulloys at
their estate in Oughtertire. Eleanor's brother, Edward O'Mulloy,
is going to marry O'Conor Don's daughter, Mary, so at least I'm
hoping to travel to Ballintober for their wedding – that is if the
O'Conors invite me.

Mary's brother, Hugh O'Conor, is the same person
father wanted me to marry – though it was before I'd even set
eyes on him. I'm sure he's the Hugh, or Aodh Eangach, referred
to in Saint Bearchán's prophesy, the man whose coming will
enable us to obtain our freedom. I visited the shrine in our castle
and promised Mary that I would say a rosary every night if she
will grant me the courage to ensure that Hugh is made King of
Connacht at Carnfree. Won't that be a wonderful day? Hugh's
father is, as you know, the direct descendant of Rory, the last
High King, but since his name is Calvagh he should not stand in
the way of Hugh's election. Don't repeat a word of this to
anybody till the time is right: there's going to be a war in Ireland

70

and it will be different from the last one because this time we'll be united.

Thomas made a poem for me before he went away:

Úna, child of my heart, I love with an aching love,
Sweet is your face in the day's life,
Sweeter your words in the straining gloom
Of the night's shore: dreams of a maiden's mind
Soothing my soul with guileless faith.

I'll tell you the rest of it when we meet again – and we will meet soon because I've told Turlough we need you now to compose more Fenian ballads like the one you wrote about our meeting with the Cootes! Anyway, little Brian and Terence need a tutor, so you could be teaching them how to read and write the way you are teaching the O'Flaherty children. I'm sure even Cathal Roe would see the benefit in that.

Do you remember Manus who helped us to remove the shrine? I met him one day in our village and he told me he's living for the time being in Ardcarn and if I wish, he'll teach me how to fight with a sword. Isn't that exciting? In Ulster he and his men used to take sheep and cattle from the Planters and those self-righteous thieves used to call them 'Tories' or 'Pursuers'. He enlisted in the army that Wentworth, Lord Strafford, raised to fight for the king but that has been disbanded. If nobody in Moylurg takes him into service he will join an Irish regiment in Flanders.

Talking of the king brings to mind our neighbours in Abbeyboyle: mother has invited John King here this evening. He's studying in Lincoln's Inn these past few years so we'll hear all about the troubles in London – not that I care a fig which of them comes out on top, Charles or Parliament, so long as they get their greedy henchmen out of Ireland. John is very earnest and tries to encourage me to read the Bible but I pretend that I can't read English. That surprises him because he knows Father

71

studied in Trinity and I speak English quite well – for a native!
He himself has only a little Irish.

You must burn this letter as soon as you've read it.
Remember what I told you about the coming war. If the Scots can
fight for their freedom, surely we can fight for ours? Wishing you
more happiness than I have and praying to Mary for your speedy
return.

From my cell in Carrick Mansion, the 4 September 1640.
Úna

"Was she very downhearted when you saw her?" I asked
Kevin.

"Not that you'd notice," he assured me. "But who knows
what goes on in a woman's head? You might as well try to
understand what a cat's thinking."

"You sound bitter," I observed.

He shrugged his shoulders: "That's what travelling does to
a man; one day I'm sweet, another bitter. Maybe I'm getting old."

"Why don't you stay in your own home then?" I said.

He gave a wry smile: "If you met my wife you'd not ask
that! You've heard of the hag Cé, how she turned into a beautiful
maiden when Oisín kissed her? Well, my beautiful maiden turned
into a scold. Take heed, scribe: beauty is a snare!"

"Where did Úna give you this letter?" I threw it on the
fire.

"Bridgeen brought it to Niall's cabin one evening after I'd
finished playing for the family." He looked at me eagerly. "Did
she say anything about my music?"

"No," I shook my head. "But I'm sure she enjoyed it just
as much as everybody here does. Have you heard her singing?"

"Yes," he said. "She sang *Roisín Dubh* for us, and it
would make you want to give your life's blood for our country's
freedom. That's a great air, slow but deep."

"Have you come across any talk of a rising on your
travels?"

"Only once. A fellow in an alehouse in Ballintober – he could have been one of Wentworth's soldiers or a Pursuer – anyway, he was reciting a prophesy about this coming year. I think it went: '*In the year Forty gorse will be without seed or bloom, and in the year following Saxons will lie stretched on the ground*' – something like that. He'd probably drunk too much bulcaan."

Whether or not there was truth in such talk, it made me more anxious than ever to be back beside Úna so that I could curb her wild enthusiasms. Little did I realise that by the very next summer my wish would be granted.

Chapter 16

Many things had changed during my absence from Cloonybrien. Turlough had brought his lame wife, Mairéad, back from Dunamon so that the atmosphere in the house was no longer free and easy. She was a pale-faced, intense woman who, while generous enough, fussed over every trifle, from the untidiness of the living room to the greasiness of the boiled meats. We had all to avoid upsetting her, and Turlough and his kernes weren't even allowed to spit on the floor when smoking. You may imagine my relief when Úna finally arrived to bring me back to Carrick Mansion. She and Mairéad greeted each other with murmurs of cordiality but it was easy to see there was no love lost between them.

Úna was somewhat warmer to me, remarking on my sunburned complexion and wondering how many hearts I'd broken in Lough Mask. I thought that she herself while no less beautiful had grown subdued and watchful, as if she were unsure whom to trust. There was a nervous intensity underlying her calm, like a sheep before it's sheared. It wasn't until we were riding away together that she spoke with some of her old spirit, teasing me about my Galway accent and wondering if I was now an expert on all the ancient learning.

"Indeed I'm not," I protested, "though they have versions of stories and poetry in West Connacht that are different from ours."

Now a thought struck me: why not tell her about a poem I had composed? Up to this moment I had never dared to hint that I loved her, fearing she would find such a revelation presumptious. Before my courage ebbed I began to recite:

> " 'Twere vain to chase the sunlight beam
> Which through the shade with golden gleam
> Moves faster than the fastest stream
> That down the mountain springs.

75

But someone may have hoped perchance,
Some fool who saw with wistful glance
It gilding lesser things,
That its quick flame, so wond'rous bright,
Might one day bathe his face in light?"

She listened smiling to the recitation then assured me it was wonderful, though I knew she considered it inferior to anything Costello had composed. A saying of my mother's came back to me: "Silence and patience gets the cat his supper." From this moment on I would keep my love for her hidden lest it only earn me her pity. In keeping with this resolve I asked about life in Carrick Mansion and she told me Eleanor had given birth to five children during my absence, three boys and two girls.

"As you can imagine, Cathal Roe would like to see me married so that they can give my room to the older boys. As always I'm just in the way."

"Oh, come now!" I remonstrated. "You're being unfair to your family."

"No, I'm not," she said. "Mother always resented the time Father spent on me. What was the point in teaching a girl Latin, Philosophy and History? She and Cathal Roe have made up their minds that I'm to marry John King. They've got Eamonn too to back them up – He's living in one of the cabins this past week."

"And how does Turlough feel about their plan?"

"Turlough is beholding to John's father: Sir Robert intervened when Turlough refused to pay Sir Charles Coote the Composition rent, otherwise he'd have been sent to prison. I think that Sir Robert himself has his eye on me – Frances, his wife, died the year after you left. He's just using John as a stalking-horse."

At the time I thought that Úna was allowing bile to poison her reason but later found that her suspicion was correct. As Eamonn explained that night in the cabin we were sharing, Sir Robert would not wish his heir to marry someone who had no fortune in land or wealth, while he himself, if he married Úna,

76

would have a beautiful young woman to comfort his remaining years.

"He's still a robust man," Eamonn said. "And even if Úna has no great dowry, she has the blood of princes in her veins, something that Sir Robert's family for all its position lacks. Don't you think it would awe those merchants up in Dublin to learn that your bride was the great-granddaughter of the King of Moylurg?"

When I brought up the question of Turlough's attitude to all this Eamonn was less forthright, though he explained that Turlough didn't see why he should pay the Composition rent if a quarter of his lands was going to be confiscated. He now went into a discussion of the legal position, from which I gathered that, while the parliament in London had just got Wentworth beheaded, the acts passed by the Dublin parliament to enable him to carry out a plantation of Connacht still stood.

"You can get John King to tell you all about the execution," he added. "He and his father are dining here tomorrow."

The following afternoon Cathal Roe, Lady Margaret, Eleanor, Úna, Honora, Eamonn and I were seated with our noble guests at the table in the Great Hall, the young children having been conveyed out of sight. In his wide-brimmed, ostrich- plumed hat, blue doublet and breeches, white lace collar and cuffs Sir Robert was an imposing figure. John, more soberly dressed in dark brown, was a handsome, if earnest young man, who kept the ladies enthralled with descriptions of life in London. While Sir Robert and Cathal Roe discussed crops and cattle, Eamonn talked to John about Saint Giles, Bow Church, Cheapside, Southwark, and other places of which I had never heard. I was about to ask if he had been present on Tower Hill when Wentworth was beheaded but feared he might not understand my rough English. However, his praise of London buildings finally moved Úna, who looked beautiful in a pale blue gown, to observe that there were magnificent stone churches and houses in Galway city, which she believed would equal anything in the Three Kingdoms.

"I've never been to Galway," John admitted, "but there's no church in Dublin that equals Westminster Abbey and compared to London Bridge with its shops and houses our bridge across the Liffey is a mere gangplank."

"Father used to tell me about a man in a play who despite his travels was always sad." Úna's eye had a mischievous twinkle. " '*All the world's a stage, and all the men and women merely players –* ' "

"Ah, *As You Like It*; the melancholy Jaques!" Eamonn interjected.

"Yes!" Úna cried. "That's his name. Are you like that person, John, dissatisfied with your own country?"

"I don't frequent the theatre." John took a sip of water. "In times like these there are more important matters to occupy us than men dressing up as women and clowns making silly jests. Actors are no better than vagabonds."

"I fancy that the present struggle between His Majesty and the Commons equals anything on the stage," Eamonn remarked. "But I must confess I enjoyed going to the Globe more than anything else in London."

"Well, John," Úna teased, "if you didn't go near the theatre, you must at least have learned to dance? Show us how to do a galliard. Come on. I'll join you."

"Now, Úna!" Lady Margaret admonished. " Let John enjoy his dinner."

"I'm afraid I was too busy with my law studies to learn dancing." John toyed with his goblet. "Perhaps you'll teach me one day?"

"Oh, I was hoping we could dance now!" Úna pouted.

"Come then, Úna!" Sir Robert exclaimed. "I'll try a measure with you. You'll see that we Kings are not as dull-spirited as you imagine."

To our amusement the two of them began to trip around the hall, Úna in her buckled shoes striving to match her steps to those of Sir John, who though over forty and in knee-high boots was surprisingly light-footed. The movement brought a rosy glow to Úna's cheeks and it was clear that despite the lack of music she was enjoying the frolic. I must confess that I felt a pang of jealousy as I watched them, for I could never hope to acquire Sir Robert's good looks and innate self-assurance. That he and Úna, who like me was twenty-six, would make a striking couple, he with his refined features and erect carriage, she with her comely face, and pale yellow hair, was like a dagger in my breast. I was almost pleased to reflect that it was neither of us but Thomas, she really wished to marry.

"I think, Úna, that's enough for now," Cathal Roe remarked.

"Yes," Lady Margaret added. "The custard pies are growing cold."

As cries of applause rang out the pair stopped dancing and bowed extravagantly to each other, then as the servant girls brought platters of cheese and griddle cakes and poured out more claret our meal continued. I had, however, lost my appetite.

Ↄ

Chapter 17

During the following days I hadn't much time to brood on Úna's apparent acceptance of Sir Robert as my work with Brian and Terence took up the greater part of the mornings and afternoons. The tutoring was conducted in the library, where Honora sometimes came to help the boys with their handwriting. She had grown more wan during my absence in Galway so that I feared any cold or ague might carry her away. It was she who revealed that Cathal Roe had invited Sir Robert to a feast, which Turlough was giving in the great hall of their castle out on the rock.

"It's in honour of King Charles and to show that Lough Key is still ours," she confided. "I also think your praising of the O'Flaherty's castle on Red Island made Turlough jealous."

"Won't this feast bring him to the attention of the Cootes?" I said.

"Turlough doesn't mind what the Cootes think so long as Sir Robert is our friend," she told me.

When I got a chance to question Úna about the feast a strange smile crossed her mouth but did not reach her eyes.

"I knew that sooner or later this would happen," she declared. "At least Father wanted me to marry John, not his father. I'm to be the pawn that saves their lands."

"Whose suggestion was it to use the castle?" I asked.

"Oh, that was Mairéad's doing," she said. "She keeps reminding Turlough of the beautiful home she had in Dunamon Castle, and of course she'd like me to be married to Sir Robert so that she'll get invited to his castle in Abbeyboyle."

"But surely Turlough wouldn't see you forced into a marriage against your wishes?"

"No, I'll grant him that. When I told him that if Thomas weren't invited to the feast I wouldn't come, he agreed to invite him. Am I wrong, Daibhí, to put my own happiness before the interests of my family?"

"That implies that your family don't care about your happiness, but from what I know of your father he loved you very much."

"Maybe, but he was weak. When certain people told him that it was important that I married somebody with riches and influence he gave in to them. If he really loved me, why couldn't he have let me choose?"

"Maybe he thought you too impulsive?" The realisation that she had never once considered me as a suitor made me speak from the head, not the heart.

"Oh, your stay in Lough Mask has turned you into a dreary, old know-all," she snapped before flouncing away.

On visits to the village during the following weeks, I occasionally saw currachs laden with furniture and draperies heading across the lough to the castle. In time two flags fluttered from poles on the battlements, the wild boar banner of the MacDermots and the red-cross banner of Saint George. Eamonn confirmed that the feast would take place after the three-day fair in July, which was held annually on level ground beside the village.

"You should have a poem composed for the occasion," he advised me, "an epithalamium for Sir Robert and his intended bride."

"Why don't you write it?" I said. "I doubt Sir Robert understands Irish."

"Maybe I'll write an address in English," he mused, pleased with my suggestion. "We must show him that we're as accomplished as any of his Dublin or London friends."

This conversation made me decide to compose a poem such as bards formerly made for their chieftains. It would be my masterpiece, proof that my years of study in Castlefore and stay in Lough Mask had not been wasted. I set to work that very night, using as a model a poem Blind Tadhg O'Huiginn had composed for his patron, Brian O'Rourke of the Ramparts, but immediately ran into difficulties. Tadhg had warned O'Rourke about going to the English court, using as a parable the story of the lion that

82

invited the other animals to his den. Now it was the MacDermots inviting Sir Robert to their castle. If everything turned out as they planned, there would be a family alliance between them and the New Gall that would protect them from the unrelenting encroachment of the Cootes. The only trouble was that Úna didn't wish to marry Sir Robert and the man she loved was probably plotting rebellion.

Night after night I wrestled with the awkward lines until inspiration struck: why not mention the wedding to Finn Mac Cumhail that King Cormac planned for his daughter Grainne? As soon as I hit on this stratagem the verses flowed. I pointed out that Cormac's wish to bind the Fianna closer to his throne had only resulted in Grainne eloping with the youthful warrior Diarmuid. This had made Finn decide to hunt them down, with the result that the Fianna were almost split in two and there was bad feeling between Cormac and Finn. There it was, no harsh words, just the implication that if Turlough wished to win Sir Robert to his side perhaps he should find another way. Of course Turlough with his half-wild kernes was more like Finn than Cormac but who would notice such a detail? Furthermore, since Sir Robert didn't speak Irish there would be no risk of offending him. I had to stop myself from composing too many verses.

Though I had swung over to Úna's side there was no opportunity to convey this, since she continued to avoid me. Now I was seeing the unforgiving side of her nature that had led to estrangement between her and her father. On the other hand, she may have kept to her room because she was convinced the whole world had turned against her. The messages I tried to send through Bridgeen were always met with the same response: she would only seek help from the Virgin since all of us were plotting against her.

My luck did not change till one evening when Honora approached me in the library just as Brian and Terence were running out for their playtime. Her appearance was gaunt and there was a feverish brightness in her eyes. After some talk about the approaching feast, she suddenly said, "Did I ever tell you that Father wrote a letter to Úna as well as to mother?"

I assured her she hadn't, whereupon she lowered her voice to a whisper: "He gave it to me to give to her after he had set out for Athlone. I was going to but then I got angry: why should he always think about her and never about me? He could see that I wasn't well but it made no difference. She was the only one he cared about. It was always like that from as long as I can remember: everybody had to be careful not to upset his darling Úna."

"Does anybody else know about this letter?" I asked.

She shook her head. "I'm only telling you because you're always kind to me. If I tell you where the letter is will you pretend that you came across it by chance?"

I nodded.

"Swear it on your soul's salvation," she added.

I did as requested, whereupon she told me to look behind Úna's portrait. When I had lifted the portrait down I found the letter wedged between the back panel and the frame. It was covered in cobwebs and the seal had been broken.

"Don't read it now," Honora begged. "Mother may come in and see you."

"Why did you decide to tell me about it today?" I couldn't help asking.

"Oh, Daibhí, can't you see that I'll be too unwell to go to the feast?" Her voice was full of pain. "If God should call me I don't want to face him with this black deed on my soul. Promise you'll think of me if...if..."

She ran from the library as the truth finally dawned on me: it was Honora and not her sister who had given me her heart.

CƷ

Chapter 18

As soon as I got back to the empty cabin I lost no time in perusing the letter. It was written in a neat, slightly old-fashioned Gaelic script, with very few corrections.

To my dear daughter, Úna

Tomorrow I set out on my journey to Athlone and unlike our last journey to Galway this one fills me with unease. Why my heart should be so heavy I cannot say. Perhaps it's because that scoundrel Black Tom Wentworth seems determined to seize a good portion of our lands – though King James granted them to me – or maybe it's because I have a premonition. Last night I dreamt that I had wandered into a dark forest from which there was no escape. People I called out to either ignored me or couldn't hear. Even you wouldn't respond because you were angry: you accused me of having turned my back on you when you needed me and said I would now know what it felt like to be deserted. That's why I'm writing this letter to you so that you'll understand that far from betraying you, as you seem to believe, I've always sought your happiness.

When did you first regard me as no longer your protector? Was it the time Rua, your pet fox, was taken away? You couldn't see that it was becoming a nuisance, attacking the hens and ducks and biting your mother's hand. You accused me of having killed it but I only got Niall to turn it loose in Knocknagapple Wood. That night I heard you crying in your room and it nearly broke my heart. Yet, wasn't it better to give your pet the freedom of the woods than to have kept him locked up in a noisome pen?

Maybe you think I should have championed you when your mother sought to bring you up as she herself had been raised, making you wear satin gowns, tying your hair with pretty lists and teaching you to do embroidery and play the lute? How could I intervene when such accomplishments were expected of any young woman of your rank? It was only when your resentment of your mother changed to violent defiance that I was obliged to restrain you. I could recount the many times when you cursed me for not taking your part in these affrays but will mention only two.

Do you remember the day you wanted to go to the fair with your brothers? You couldn't see that what might be all right for scullogues' daughters and village girls might not be all right for someone in your position. You became so angry that it was necessary to lock you in your room. The following year I did permit you to join the revellers at our bonfire on Saint John's Eve, though you were furious when your mother and I took you home before midnight. You felt that if it was all right for your brothers to be there then it should be all right for you. Now that you are grown up surely you can understand that we would wish to shield our daughter from idle talk? It's not enough to point out that we were treating you differently from Bryan and Teige who were with you – and who if, I recall correctly, had drunk more usquebagh than they should. In these matters young men aren't judged as harshly as girls.

Which brings me to another point. Of all my children I feel that whatever spark of talent I possess has been passed on to you. That is why I have such hopes that you will marry somebody who will appreciate your gifts and give you the leisure to cultivate your mind instead of simply bearing children. It was with this object in mind that I proposed Calvagh O'Conor's son, Hugh, as a suitable husband, for like us the O'Conors Dons have always been patrons of learning.

I won't harp on what's past, but my wish that since Hugh had been betrothed to another girl you should consider marrying John King was, before everything else, born of the same thinking. John is a Dubliner, educated in Cambridge and heir to our neighbour, Sir Robert. You chose to believe that I was only looking out for our family's advantage and I won't deny that that was a consideration. The lands of Boyle Abbey, which the Kings now own, was once part of the Kingdom of Moylurg and an alliance between our two families, while it would not reunify this ancient territory would at least forge bonds between its owners. Furthermore, what benefits our family benefits you. In these dangerous times we need the friendship of those who can protect us from the snares of our enemies.

If my years in Trinity taught me anything it is that the days when we were masters of our own destiny are gone forever. When our poets recite poems about Naoise and Deirdre or Oisín and Niamh they are dreaming of the old Gaelic world that died at Kinsale. For good or ill we are now beholden to the New Gall, people who are ruled by their heads, not their hearts. If we don't accommodate ourselves to this change we are doomed. Remember I was a ward of court so I know what it is to be dependent on others. That's why I wish you to marry John King, who will, I'll be bound, prove a kind, sober husband. You will rightly point out that he's a Lutheran but just as His Majesty respects the beliefs of his dear wife, Henrietta Maria, I'm sure John will respect yours. Indeed it is more likely that my clever daughter will entice him away from the Reformed Church than that he will entice her away from Rome.

Now I'll grant that you have convinced yourself that you are in love with another man, a landless adventurer whose claim to fame seems to rest on his physical prowess and ability to compose street ballads. Such reckless gallants may turn the heads of milkmaids but can hardly be considered ideal husbands. Indeed the man in question is reputed to have left many a young woman disgraced, though these, I'll admit, are stories that are not easily confirmed. If you can choose such a scapegrace before a suitor such as John King you are, it grieves me to say, betraying that enlightened mind with which your birth and upbringing endowed you.

Well, Úna, that's all I have time to write. If I thought I would always be here to shield you I would not express these admonitions. You are as dear to me as my heart's pulse and when you accuse me of being led in these matters by self-interest or your mother's high notions, you ignore what I have always felt

for you and will continue to feel, no matter how you upbraid me.
If we could only get back the bright, young girl that once lit up
our house with her smiling face I would swap places with the
poorest beggar in Ireland.

God keep and shield you,
Dadda.

When I finished reading the letter I was in a quandary, not knowing whether to show it to Úna at once or to wait till after the feast. It struck me that what Brian Oge wanted, a marriage alliance with the Kings, ran counter to what I was counselling in my poem. On the other hand, he had the youthful John King, not Sir Robert, in mind for his daughter. What would he advocate if he were alive? Would he refuse his beloved daughter's hand to this widower or would he prefer such a man, despite his age, to Thomas Costello? Unable to find an answer, I decided to let chance determine the outcome. If Úna deigned to speak to me I would show her the letter; if she didn't, why burden her further with its unasked-for advice? So it was that events moved on to their fateful conclusion.

છ

Chapter 19

If the feast in the great hall of Carrick MacDermot could not boast as many noble guests and men of learning as those described in the Annals it was still the most splendid that I had ever seen or am likely to see. Tapestries, one showing a stag hunt, another knights and their ladies, another Solomon greeting the Queen of Sheba, decorated the bare walls and candles on tall wooden standards filled the place with mellow light. At the raised table before the narrow recessed window Úna sat with Cathal Roe and Eleanor on her right and Lady Margaret and Eamonn on her left. To my surprise Turlough was not at the centre of the table but instead was seated with his wife Mairéad at the north end, facing Sir Robert and his agent, Tom Hewett, at the opposite end.

The rest of us, including retainers of the MacDermots and *scullogues* in their grey frieze jerkins, had been placed on either side of a long trestle table presided over by Úna's brother, Teige, a handsome, tawny-haired young man. This trestle table formed a T with the raised table, both of which were laden with platters of food, goblets of claret and *meadars* of ale. Eithne and Siobhan trailed by Turlough's wolfhounds hurried here and there with *sciatháns* of mutton and oaten cakes while village boys carried leather jugs of wine and pitchers of ale to refill our drinking vessels. At one side Niall Dall was sitting on a low stool near the fireplace playing *geantraí* or merry tunes on his harp, his blind eyes closed in concentration. If only Father Bernard were there to say Grace we might have been back in the unfettered days before the Composition of Connacht but with two New Gall present, he had to keep out of sight.

Though those at the raised table were in sumptuous attire, Úna dressed in a blue velvet gown with a white lace collar stood out like a lone cornflower growing among poppies, ox-eye daisies and buttercups. I had never seen her look so mild and radiant as if her beauty, usually clouded by doublet and breeches, was at last shining forth in all its fullness. Thomas must have noticed this too as from his position between Bridgeen and Niall at the end of the trestle table he seemed to devour her with his eyes. I had no doubt that Cathal Roe had asked Niall and Bridgeen to sit near him so that they might calm him should he grow resentful of Sir Robert.

Lee the Healer and Nora his wife were on one side of me, and Turlough's man, Rory, on the other so that I had to converse with them while worrying lest I should forget some of my *ranns* or worse, that the poem itself might anger Turlough. Finally, to allay my anxiety, I pretended that I was going to visit the garderobe then once outside searched for the oratory. One of Turlough's kernes standing in the passageway, armed with a hazel staff, pointed to a door and I went through into a small chamber lit by an oil lamp burning on a stone altar.

Once my eyes became adjusted to the dim interior I saw that the shrine, which had been fitted into the wall above the altar, had been painted: Mary was now wearing blue garments and the child Jesus purple ones. On the right a painted wooden panel showed a monk in a white habit gazing up at the shrine and another on the left showed the Annunciation with Mary again in a blue gown and Gabriel in white with gold-tipped wings. If some foreign artist had painted the monk then his work had been far outstripped by Úna's lifelike rendering of the Virgin and Angel.

I knelt on a prie-dieu, blessed myself and begged the Virgin to assist me so that I would be able to recite my poem before the gathering. Then to my amazement I saw tears flowing down her cheeks. When I begged her to reveal the reason for her distress a voice inside my head answered, "Don't you realise that Úna is with child? That is why she has kept to her room these past weeks. You must ensure that she does not marry this man who denies me." Even today I can't tell if what I experienced in that oratory was real. Perhaps it was the uncertain light from the lamp that was playing tricks on me? Whatever the truth of the matter, I returned to the feast resolved to speak out against Úna's betrothal to Sir Robert.

When I re-entered the Great Hall bowls of troander had been set before us and Cathal Roe was on his feet addressing the guests in English. I don't recall much of what he said but I do remember him assuring us that his father always maintained that a mixing of bloodlines was most beneficial. Their own family, the MacDermots, were both Gaelic and Norman, or as the people would say, Milesian and Old Gall. Now the time had come to forge bonds of kinship between them and the New Gall, among whom his distinguished visitors from Abbeyboyle must be reckoned. He praised Sir Robert for his generous assistance to the family in the recent troubled times and hoped that soon there would be an even closer bond between their two houses.

Sir Robert was about to rise when Thomas, who had obviously drunk too freely, jumped up and began declaiming in Gaelic:

> *Lapwings cry over wet fields,*
> *Thatch eaves drip, and hawthorns pluck*
> *From the wind's harp a weary sighing:*
> *Sad is Moylurg tonight,*
>
> *The lights from cabin doors too few and faint*
> *To warm the ghost wand'ring its rutted lanes.*
> *Where is the head of gold that blazed against*
> *The summer fields of skylark-songed Moylurg,*
>
> *Where is the bright blue eye?*
> *The dark ghost wanders through the empty lanes,*
> *While far away a castle's glow*
> *Defeats the night.*

Though the poem did not observe the rules of metre and rhyme, it was delivered with such pathos that those at our table burst into loud applause and at the raised table Úna smiled her pleasure. When the shouting and clapping died down Sir Robert made a gracious speech in which he regretted his inability to address us in Gaelic and referred to his dead brother Edward, a cleric and poet, who had told him that the great Spenser had praised the compositions of the Irish bards. He had one of

Spenser's sonnets, which dealt with Phoebus's pursuit of Daphne and which, with our indulgence, he would like to read out. He then took a sheet from his doublet and looking from it to Úna began to recite. If memory serves me it ended with the couplet:

> Then fly no more, fair love, from Phoebus chase,
> But in your breast his leaf and love embrace.

When he finished there was warm applause from the upper table but only polite clapping from ours, many of those around me having no English. I saw Úna bow graciously to Sir Robert but don't know how Thomas reacted since I was casting a final glance over my own poem. It was now Turlough's turn to speak. An expectant hush fell on the hall as he got slowly to his feet. Expressing himself with less fluency but more real warmth than Cathal Roe, he thanked us all in English, especially Sir Robert and Tom Hewett, for honouring the family with our presence. His father, Brian Oge, would be pleased if he were there since he always hoped to see the castle restored to its old glory as the Oxford of Connacht. In this regard Eamonn had informed him that I, the family's ollave, had prepared a praise poem, which he would now call on me to deliver.

Having thus avoided any allusion to the true purpose of the feast he sat down amid boisterous applause and all eyes turned to me. My throat was dry and my palms sweating. Signalling to Niall Dall to accompany me on the harp I began to recite. At first there was no indication that my listeners understood the warning about the intended betrothal but soon I could see Cathal Roe's brow darkening as the words struck home. On the other hand, Úna's face lit up with pleasure and Thomas got so carried away that, when I finally sat down to cries of "Goirm thu!" and "Rath Dé ort!" he launched into the song "Eibhlín a Rún", in which the singer begs the girl Eibhlín to flee with him from her father's castle and she agrees. To make matters worse Úna made no effort to conceal her delight and when Thomas finished the crowd shouted its appreciation. As for Sir Robert since he didn't understand the words he joined good-humouredly in the applause.

It was at this point that Turlough, urged on by his wife Mairéad, sent one of the serving boys to me with a goblet of wine. By this gesture he acknowledged the merit of my poem while ignoring Thomas's song. If only that had been the end of the matter...

ᴄꙅ

Chapter 20

There were now two opposing groups in the hall, those at the upper table who favoured a marriage between Úna and Sir Robert and those at our table, with the possible exception of her brother Teige, who sympathised with Thomas. Of course there may have been some like myself who didn't want her to choose either the suave, imposing widower or the hot headed, half-wild Mayo man. It was at this juncture that Cathal Roe whispered something to Eamonn, who rose to address us.

With a lawyer's fluency, Eamonn praised Sir Robert for his moderation in the Dublin parliament and his refusal to toady to the newly appointed Puritan lords justices, Parsons and Borlase. In this time when there were rumours that the Scots intended to crush Catholicism by force we were fortunate to have such a distinguished champion representing Abbeyboyle. He understood the desire of some people to see young love triumph over sense and reason, but the stories of Deirdre and Naoise or Romeo and Juliet should warn us that such headstrong surges of passion always end in grief – A low growl from Thomas greeted this remark but Eamonn ignored it. He himself had suffered the pangs of passion in his youth and blamed his father for thwarting its fulfilment. Today he could see that his father's opposition had saved him from the consequences of an unequal alliance. As the Roman poet Ovid so well expressed it, *Credula res amor est:* Love is a credulous thing.

It was clear that these remarks were intended for Úna's ears but if Thomas understood their full import they must have galled him. Sir Robert, on the other hand, sipped his wine as though the matter were none of his concern. When Eamonn referred to those, such as his own people, the Burkes, who had over time become *Hibernis hiberniores,* Irish of the Irish, and hoped that this was about to happen again, Sir Robert stroked his pointed beard while an amused smile played about his mouth. Finally, Eamonn referred to the lovely English air, "Greensleeves", which Niall Dall had picked up after he had whistled it to him a few times and which he now hoped he would play for their distinguished visitors.

Eamonn's speech met with warm applause from the upper table but since many guests did not understand English, it required encouraging glances from Teige to get the rest of us to display enthusiasm. Niall Dall's rendering of "Greensleeves" – which I had never heard till then – was declared by Sir Robert to be unbeatable. Cathal Roe told him that it had been one of their father's favourite songs and asked Úna to sing it. At first she refused but pressed by Sir Robert agreed, if Teige would join her. How lovely she looked with her head thrown back as she and Teige, facing each other, poured out the sad-sweet lines that echoed my own thoughts:

> *Thy gown was of the grassy green,*
> *Thy sleeves of satin hanging by,*
> *Which made of thee a harvest queen,*
> *And yet thou wouldst not love me.*

The contrast between Teige's deep tones and her warbling ones enchanted us all and I could see Sir Robert swaying his head in time to the chorus.

No sooner had the sustained applause died down than Thomas was on his feet begging Úna to sing "*Fol-i-ó-hó-ró*" with him. Signalling to her to ignore the request, Cathal Roe, his voice slurred with wine, said it was now time to drink to the health of our guests. We raised our drinking vessels as he intoned, "To our honoured guests, Sir Robert and Tom Hewett: *Sláinte!*" then having responded with, "*Sláinte agus saol fada!*" we swallowed our claret or ale, only Thomas leaving his meadar untouched. Sir Robert now called on us to drink to the health of the MacDermot family, in particular their lovely daughter, Úna. His use of the word "*Sláinte*" instead of "Health" pleased everybody except Thomas, who sat motionless like a wounded bull. With a sense of unease I half drained my goblet of claret just as Cathal Roe

96

began: "I will now call on Úna to drink to the health of the man she likes best in this company."

Úna stood up, looked from Thomas to Sir Robert, then back again, hesitated a moment, finally in a clear voice said, "I drink to the health of Thomas Costello."

No sooner were the words uttered than the back of Cathal Roe's left hand struck her face, knocking her goblet to the floor. Immediately consternation filled the hall, many of those at our table calling out, "*Fubún!* Shame!" With a stricken cry Thomas shouted, "I'll kill him!"

Forgetting his superior strength, I immediately told him in a loud voice: "No, you won't! Do you want to hurt her more?"

"Let go!" Thomas broke away from Niall, who was trying to restrain him and made for the raised table, his scian in his hand. Teige blocked his way.

"Listen," I ran up to Thomas, "do you want the foreigners to tell everyone we Gaels are no better than savages? If you lay a hand on Cathal Roe I swear to you I'll write a satire than will follow you to your dying day."

Whether it was this threat or his reluctance to strike Teige I don't know but Thomas returned to his seat just as Úna picked up a small snuff box and, to our amazement, slowly and deliberately took a pinch. Now it was common enough for men and older women to use snuff but Úna must have borrowed Eamonn's in order to cover up her tears. I was proud of her spirit as she stood there trying to remain dignified while Cathal Roe sat beside her, hands clasped over his head with remorse. Turlough whispered something to Lady Margaret and presently she and Eleanor led Úna from the hall.

At this juncture Sir Robert rose also and thanking the MacDermots for their hospitality, said that in view of the late hour he and Tom Hewett must be setting out for Abbeyboyle. Hearing this, Teige asked me in a low voice to get Thomas away first. Throwing caution aside, I walked down to the end of the table.

"Look, Thomas," I said, "Úna drank to your health. For her sake, let you and I leave before the New Gall. If you stay it will only create more bad feeling."

He looked at me with tears in his eyes, then without a word rose and the two of us walked out to the passageway, where Thomas retrieved two saddlebags from a peg. Feeling our way step by step down the winding stone stairs, we strode along passages lit by bog deal torches, past a room where some of Turlough's kernes were carousing and out into the cool dusk of the bawn. The porter grumbled as he opened the small, iron door, asking were we Lutherans that we were in such a hurry to leave a feast. When we descended to the currachs, Thomas instead of getting into one began to strip off his clothes.

"What are you doing?" I didn't hide my amazement.

"Do you think I'll be beholding to people who treat me like an outcast?" he snapped. "I don't need anything from the MacDermots."

Rolling his clothes into bundles, he stuffed them together with his brogues into the saddlebags then slung the bags over his back with the strap about his neck.

"Won't your clothes get wet?" I persisted.

"They won't," he declared, "and, anyway, the water will wash the stench of this night off me – To think Úna's people would fawn like that before New Gall!"

Carefully he lowered himself into the water then, moving his arms and legs like a frog, swam away from the castle and was soon swallowed up in the darkness.

ABRIDGED FAMILY TREES

The O'Conors of Magh Aí:

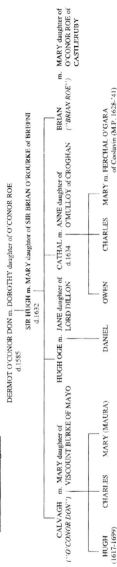

DERMOT O'CONOR DON m. DOROTHY daughter of O'CONOR ROE
d.1585

SIR HUGH m. MARY daughter of SIR BRIAN O'ROURKE of BREFNI
d.1632

CALVAGH m. MARY daughter of
("O'CONOR DON") VISCOUNT BURKE OF MAYO

HUGH OGE m. JANE daughter of
LORD DILLON

CATHAL m. ANNE daughter of
d.1634 O'MULLOY of CROGHAN

BRIAN
("BRIAN ROE") m. MARY daughter of
O'CONOR ROE of
CASTLERUBY

HUGH
(1617-1699)

CHARLES

MARY (MAURA)

DANIEL

OWEN

CHARLES

MARY m. FERCHAL O'GARA
of Coolavin (M.P. 1628-'41)

The MacDermots of Moylurg:

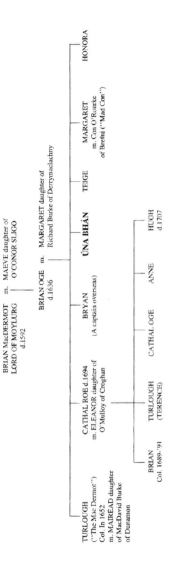

BRIAN MacDERMOT
LORD OF MOYLURG
d.1592

m. MAEVE daughter of
O'CONOR SLIGO

BRIAN OGE m. MARGARET daughter of
d.1636 Richard Burke of Derrymaclachtny

TURLOUGH
("The Mac Dermot")
Col. In 1652
m. MAIREAD daughter
of MacDavid Burke
of Duramon

CATHAL ROE d.1694
m. ELEANOR daughter of
O'Mulloy of Croghan

BRYAN
(A captain overseas)

ÚNA BHÁN

TEIGE

MARGARET
m. Con O'Rourke
of Brefni ("Mad Con")

HONORA

BRIAN
Col 1689-'91

TURLOUGH
(TERENCE)

CATHAL OGE

ANNE

HUGH
d.1707

99

The Kings of Abbeyboyle

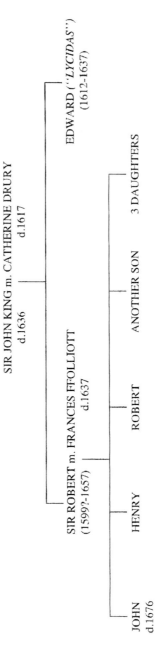

SIR JOHN KING m. CATHERINE DRURY
d.1636   d.1617

EDWARD ("*LYCIDAS*")
(1612-1637)

SIR ROBERT m. FRANCES FFOLLIOTT
(1599?-1657)   d.1637

JOHN
d.1676

HENRY

ROBERT

ANOTHER SON

3 DAUGHTERS

Chapter 21

That night brought calamity not only to Thomas and Úna but to me also. Though I had recited a well-made poem filled with sound advice and played my part in steering Thomas away from bloodshed, Cathal Roe could not forget that I had opposed the marriage to Sir Robert. In an hour of danger for the family I had chosen to put his sister's happiness before the family's welfare. He made some excuse about the boys having had enough tutoring in Gaelic, paid me for the time I had spent with them and loaned me a garron for the journey home to Kilmactranny. When I asked to say farewell to Úna he told me she had taken to her bed with a fever and was not well enough to receive visitors.

So it was that after bidding farewell to the MacDermot household, including Honora, who cried as we shook hands, I rode away from Carrick Mansion with a heavy heart and set out for the bridge at Knockvicar. Had I but known it, there were worse things in store for me and the country than the misfortunes of that hour but praise be to God and His Holy Mother that keeps the future hidden from us.

When I was a few miles beyond Crossna my mood lightened. It had been five years since I had said goodbye to my own family and I was telling myself that they would be delighted to see me and I could help Philip with the hay saving. While trotting downhill I encountered a small gully cut across the trackway by torrents, which I carelessly urged the garron to jump. He landed on loose stones and fell on me before struggling to his feet. After a few moments I recovered my breath but on attempting to rise found that my left leg was powerless. On touching it my hand came away covered in blood. It was now close to sunset; there was nobody about and I was miles from home. You can imagine the thoughts that went through my mind, in particular how I cursed myself for not having dismounted before crossing the gully.

My mother had a saying, "God's help is nearer than the door," and so it turned out. After half an hour lying there, a scullogue coming from the bog with his garron and turf sled found me. He partly unloaded the sled, helped me onto it, tied my garron's reins to the side rail and brought me to his cabin. Since this account is about Úna I won't dwell on all that man and his family did for a stranger, except to relate that next morning he carried me, tossed and jolted, on his sled all the way to my own home, refusing to take one penny for his trouble. Mother sent Philip for the bonesetter and when he had fixed a splint to my thigh, she and Eileen cared for me like an infant. By evening, however, my leg was racked with pain and I had become feverish.

It was two months before I could walk again and then only with a limp. That, and not from any battle wound, is how I got my sobriquet, "Lame Daibhí". If my hopes of winning Úna had been meagre before, what were they now? Nevertheless, like some foolish dream, they persisted. Maybe it was as well that I was unable to ride back to Carrick Mansion with the garron because one day Rory arrived to fetch him.

"How is Úna?" I asked as soon as he dismounted.

"You haven't heard then?" he replied. "She went the night Honora, God rest her soul, passed away. That was over five weeks ago and nobody has laid eyes on her since."

You can imagine my shock on hearing these terrible tidings. After pressing him for a fuller account, he confided, "Between you and me the family think the poor girl drowned herself in the lough but I wouldn't mention a word of that to anyone else. They don't want Costello to blacken their name further."

When Rory had finished the meal of oaten cakes, cheese, watercress and buttermilk that mother and Eileen set before him he lit his pipe and told us what Bridgeen had told him.

The night of the feast Úna had developed a fever. Even though the family got Lee the Healer, to treat her she wouldn't drink his simples or eat anything. Finally in desperation they were obliged to send to Tullaghanmore for Costello. When he arrived Bridgeen brought him to Úna's room but the family, not wishing to hear any accusations, avoided him. His visit seemed to revive

Úna. She asked Bridgeen for food and drink and then fell into a peaceful sleep. What nobody realised was that Costello had left the house furious at the cold reception he had been given. It seems he and his servant waited in a ford of the River Donogue to see if the family would call him back. Meanwhile Úna woke up and found him gone. She grew frantic so Cathal Roe sent one of his horseboys after Costello but when he reached the ford Thomas was already on the far bank. He told the horseboy he had sworn that if he were not sent for before he crossed the river he would return to Mayo. That night Honora, who had been ailing, passed away so, with all the preparations for the wake, nobody was keeping a close watch on Úna. When Bridgeen went to her room later in the night she was gone.

"And you've no idea what happened to the poor creature?" my mother asked.

"That's all I can tell you," Rory declared. "The family have asked after her in every parish in the county but nobody has seen or heard anything."

"Well, glory be to God," Eileen broke in. "Isn't that the saddest tale, two lovely sisters lost in the one night?"

"It is that," Rory agreed, pleased with the warmth of her response. "Sure they were only about your own age."

Eileen blushed under his admiring gaze and began to wash the dishes.

"That Costello must be a hard-hearted devil," my mother said. "Oh, I know he felt slighted, but to put his own pride before the happiness of the poor girl... Sure for all her wearing of men's clothes and arguing with Father Malachy she was the kindest and least conceited person that ever set foot in this house."

"Ah, Costello is just a brawler and landless upstart who thinks too highly of himself," Rory remarked.

"Still, he comes from no mean family," I pointed out, "and he himself is a true poet."

"A true poet is it?" Rory snorted. "Sure the poem you yourself recited at the feast is far ahead of anything he ever made.

You should have heard the way we raised the rafters with our cheering," he told Eileen, increasing her confusion.

To my anguish at the tale Rory brought us was added remorse for not having given Úna her father's letter. Nevertheless I clung to the hope that she was still alive and that if I searched the length and breadth of Ireland I would one day find her. She might even have gone overseas to join her brother, Bryan.

As soon as the harvest was gathered in and my lame leg felt strong enough I ventured north on Philip's garron. This sturdy beast kept up a steady pace that brought us after four hours' travel to the MacDonagh castle at Collooney, where, over forty years previously, my father had taken part in the great siege. Nobody in the castle had seen Úna, so next day I continued on to Sligo town.

There being no wall about the town I was able to enter unchallenged, though a beige-coated sentry with crossed shoulder straps, one holding wooden powder pods, the other a sword which almost touched the ground, stared at me while leaning on his musket. Avoiding his eyes I rode slowly up the cobbled street between wooden-framed houses, most of which were thatched, though some had brown-tiled roofs. Somberly dressed men wearing high-crowned hats and housewives in dark gowns with white linen kerchiefs covering their hair stood conversing or picked their way past garrons with loaded panniers and horse-drawn wagons, while urchins gawked at a greasy-haired youth sitting in the stocks with a notice, "Cutpurses Take Heed", tied to his neck. Everybody was speaking loudly in English, while a number of amazons standing by wheelbarrows shouted in the same tongue: "Apples a penny a peck"; "Herrings alive, alive here" and other such catchcries.

In the midst of this babble the mournful sound of a *geocach's* voice caught my attention. Dismounting, I walked towards the market square, which was filled with my own kind, a crowd of half-ragged Gaels. As my halting gait took me

104

closer to the young man the words of his song became clear, sending shivers up my spine:

"Úna Bhán, flower of the amber tresses,
You who have met death because of bad counsel;
Look, my love, which was the better of the two counsels,
Bird in a cage and I in the ford of the Donogue?"

There was such wild grief in the words that I knew they had to be composed by Thomas, a belief that was confirmed later in the Boar's Head, an alehouse near Saint John's Church, where I brought the *geocach* to share my dinner of grilled herrings. He told me that he had heard Thomas singing the song in Ballaghaderreen. He didn't know who Úna Bhán was but thought she might be somebody with whom Costello had been in love. Her people must have been rich because one of the ranns spoke about those "who throw disrespect upon an empty estate" but he had no idea who they might be. I asked him how Thomas looked and he said that if you ever saw a trapped wolf you would have a good idea; one minute you would feel pity for him and the next he might turn and sink his teeth in your throat.

Distracted by his account and confused by too many meadars of usquebagh I decided to walk round the town to clear my head. About fifty yards past a gloomy strong-house with two armed warders standing by the entrance and the red cross banner of Saint George flying from its battlement, a woman hardly older than myself, smiled at me. Her large dark eyes and drawn face showed a ravaged beauty. When I smiled back she addressed me in English, saying that for one shilling she would take me to her lodgings. Lust driving all thoughts of Úna from my head I paid what she asked and followed her at a distance, she being anxious that nobody should see us walking together. Once in her bleak, windowless room, she lit a candle, placed it on the floor by a pallet covered with threadbare blankets, put more turf sods on the smouldering fire and told me to strip. As I removed my garments one by one she did likewise, filling me with desire. Her body had escaped the changes which marred her face, so that, naked, she seemed a pagan goddess, high bosomed and smooth limbed.

Like a man in a scorched desert who chances on a well, I drank deeply of her abundance, giving no thought to my soul or body's danger. Two or three times I returned to her embrace, while she, stroking my head and calling me 'Husband', sought to have me kiss her mouth, something that the thought of Úna would not let me do. Though I denied her this request I could not help thinking that if we had met before her fall I would have gladly consented, for she was a kind, well-spoken woman. She told me that four years previously she had come from Bristol with the son of a Roscommon chieftan who had promised to marry her. His father, however, had made him cast her off. Now she hoped to earn enough money to return home, that is if she escaped the vigilance of Reverend Newport, the minister in Saint John's church, who had denounced her from the pulpit as a harlot.

"Who was the chieftain's son who cast you off?" I lay on one arm beside her.

"Donogh O'Beirne from ... Cheerbrun – I can't pronounce those Gaelic names. Have you heard of him?"

I told her 'No' and then asked why his father had rejected her.

"O'Beirne wanted Donogh to wed someone rich and highborn who would add to the family's standing and my father was only a glover, though an honest one... He said I was a harlot, yet, as God's my judge, I was a maid when I met his son."

If she was a harlot, I reflected, it was one like Mary Magdalen, a person God would forgive because she had loved much. As for myself there could be no such excuse. Had I not sullied my soul when I should have been thinking of Úna? To salve my conscience I gave her another shilling then when she had peeped out the door to confirm that the way was clear, I bade her goodbye and hurried away.

There was now a canker in my soul that demanded purging, so instead of repairing to a pallet in the Boar's Head I walked back by the warders guarding the strong-house and on past merchants' homes, searching for the abbey. A man carrying a creel of turf, whose features proclaimed him a fellow Gael, told me the abbey had been turned into a barracks but that two friars were now living in a cabin near the Garravogue River. Following his directions I soon found the cabin. Kneeling on the earthen floor beside a chair on which a frail, white-haired Dominican sat, I confessed my many sins. He upraided me for my sordid indulgence before shriving me, then having listened to my account of Úna, he told me never to give up my quest for her.

"We know that with God all things are possible," he said. "If nobody has seen her dead body, why then you must continue your search. Remember how Joseph and Mary once feared Jesus was lost, yet after searching for three days they found him safe in the temple."

Chapter 22

Next morning before rising I began to go over in my mind how Úna, if she were still alive, might have got away without being discovered. At once it occurred to me that somebody must have helped her – but who could that be? Turlough's home in Cloonybrien had been her refuge in the past but Mairéad or Eamonn would have told Cathal Roe if she were hiding there. Suddenly, like a flash, the answer came: it had to be Teige. I recalled their singing of "*Greensleeves*" and the letters in which she had written of his promise to take her overseas to join their brother, Bryan. Teige was now steward for the O'Mulloys in Oughtertire, which was only a short distance northeast of Cloonybrien. If I went there I would be almost certain to find news of her.

I was leading the garron down the cobbled street past the Gaol House when the music of pipes drew me to the market square. Who should be playing to the delighted crowd but Kevin who used to visit O'Flaherty's castle! It was almost half an hour before I was able to talk to him while he was gathering up scattered farthings. When I asked if he had seen Úna during his travels he put on a sad look. Hadn't I heard that she had died?

"She's not dead," I assured him and I could see from his guarded expression that he knew it too. Úna must have sworn him to secrecy.

"Listen," I said, "I'll write a letter to her and if you come upon her in your travels, will you give it to her?"

"It'll be like looking for a mare's nest," he warned, "but seeing, Scribe, as how you and I shared many a meadar of usquebagh in Red Island, I'll try."

Thanking him profusely, I returned to the alehouse, paid the churlish landlord two pennies for a sheet of paper, sealing wax and a quill and hastily wrote:

To "Greensleeves"

I have a letter that your father wrote to you before he went to Athlone. If you write to me I will send it to you and not tell anybody where you are staying. I am back in Tirerrill till somebody needs a scribe or tutor.

God and Mary shield you. D.

I folded the sheet and sealed it then hurried back to the market square. Since he could not admit that there would be somebody to whom he could give it, Kevin agreed to take the letter with him for a sixpenny piece. If he brought an answer I was to give him another sixpence. As we shook hands he remarked with a wry grin, "I thought that woman of mine was persistent but she'd not hold a candle to yourself."

"Persistence got the spider up the wall," I reminded him before limping away. Feeling more hopeful than I had in ages, I rode out of Sligo, heading back southwards.

Two days later, having rested at home to ease an ache in my bad leg, I hailed Teige as he was fishing from a currach on Lough Eidin, not far from the O'Mulloys' house in Oughtertire. He was pleased to see me and invited me to join him. While I manned the oars, he took up a rod and line on which there was a hook concealed under two or three flies. As we moved along the reed-fringed water in the stillness of the afternoon I brought the conversation round to Úna. Did he miss his sister much? He looked at me closely then said, "I'd prefer not to discuss that."

From his uneasy expression I knew my intuition that he had helped her flee from Carrick Mansion was correct.

"Listen, Teige," I said, "I know Úna is alive and I have no intention of ever revealing her whereabouts to Cathal Roe or anybody else, but Honora, God rest her, gave me a letter which your father wrote to Úna before he travelled to Athlone. If she reads that letter it may prove that he did not turn his back on her as she believes."

"Can I see the letter?" he asked.

"No," I said. "It was meant for Úna's eyes alone."

110

"But you and Honora read it," he pointed out.

"That may be so," I agreed. "Nevertheless, as Úna's friend I won't let others see it without her permission, not even you. I know you and she were close but she told me you promised to take her with you to the Spanish Netherlands and you didn't."

"I did that to humour her," he confessed. "Úna gets wild notions into her head and thinks that anybody who doesn't go along with them is against her. She listens to that hothead, Manus – I mean she used to listen to him."

"Is he the Manus that was staying in Ardcarn?"

"Yes, Manus Maguire. He's a Pursuer from Fermanagh, ready for any desperate enterprise. The latest is a war against the New Gall."

We discussed the rumours of an uprising but decided that after the defeat of Kinsale very few people would take part in a new one.

"Though Úna mightn't agree with us," I remarked.

Whatever reply Teige was about to make was cut short when a large trout took his bait. Thereafter he had to concentrate on playing and landing the fish.

Teige cooked the trout over a fire of dry sticks and we ate it with oaten cakes, drinking ale from goatskins, while sitting on the ground like two ancient Fenians. He had Úna's winning ways and seeing that I was determined to continue my search for her, promised he would make enquiries on my behalf.

"But it may all be labour in vain," he warned. "She's very far from here."

Not wishing to press him further I said it was time for me to go. On hearing this he invited me to spend the night in his small, thatched house beside the O'Mulloy's partly built, two-storied mansion. Before retiring, we sat by the fire drinking usquebagh and talked about the prophesies of another war and his regret that he had not joined his brother in the Spanish Netherlands; Bryan had met Owen Roe, a nephew of the famous Hugh O'Neill, who was renowned out there for defending Arras

111

against the French. There were even rumours that Owen Roe was planning to free Ireland.

Early next morning I took my leave of Teige but, yielding to a sudden impulse, crossed the Boyle River at Knockvicar and skirting Cloonybrien rode on south to Ardcarn, a cluster of mud and wattle cabins surrounding a roofless priory. At first nobody would admit that they had ever known Manus but when I told them that I had been scribe and tutor for the MacDermots and that my kinsman, Philip Ballach, had lived at Cloonybrien, one old man who remembered him invited me into his cabin, where his wife pressed me to take a fresh griddle cake and buttermilk.

While I ate my host told me that Manus had stayed on and off in the village *shebeen* but had disappeared at the end of July or the beginning of August. There were those who said he had set out for the North one night with a youthful companion but with a man like Manus you wouldn't know what to believe. In the *shebeen* he used to meet with strangers and they would huddle in a corner drinking *meadars* of ale. Úna had been with him a few times but she always rode back to Carrick Mansion on her own – that was earlier in the summer, weeks before the poor girl and her sister, Lord have mercy on them both, had caught the fever which killed them.

I was now more convinced than ever that Úna was alive and had probably travelled to the North with Manus, so offering the kind old couple a groat for their hospitality, an offer they indignantly refused, I rode away from Ardcarn and, though my bad leg ached with the strain, was home before nightfall.

To while away the time while waiting for word from Teige or a letter from Kevin I helped Philip bring home the turf and cut *scollops* to thatch the roof. At other times I rode to the plain of Moytirra where the Tuatha Dé Dananns had defeated the Fomorians or further west to the caves of Keshcorran where Diarmuid and Grainne hid for a time from Finn, talking to old people about those glorious far-off days when Tara was the capital of Ireland and the Fenian warriors protected us from invaders. Nevertheless, week after week went by with nothing to show that Úna was aware of my growing anxiety.

C03

Chapter 23

Samhain, that festival when Otherworld spirits are unleashed on the living, came and went; then one day in late November Rory arrived. You could see from his face that he had something exciting to relate. Drawing me to one side he handed me a letter from Teige, which said that because of the stories of an uprising in Ulster he was at the earliest opportunity travelling to Cavan town in East Breifne to bring Úna home. If I wished to join him I was to return to Oughtertire with Rory. Meanwhile it would be Úna's earnest wish that I should tell nobody about her whereabouts or reveal that she was still alive.

Over dinner Rory told us that Turlough had learned that at the end of October a number of northern chieftains, including Lord Conor Maguire of Fermanagh, had been arrested in Dublin for plotting to capture the castle. That same night a rising led by Sir Phelim O'Neill had taken place in Ulster and the whole province was now in flames. He himself was determined to travel to East Breifne to join in the fighting.

"Won't that be dangerous?" Eileen looked troubled.

"What do I care about danger if I can get our land back," Rory replied. "It's close to Lough Ramor, the best grazing in South Ulster. Father used to tell us how O'Neill gathered his army on the hill opposite our house before marching down to Kinsale; fifteen hundred footsoldiers and two hundred horsemen he had. You'd love living there, Eileen, with its green hills and the great shining lough before it."

Eileen blushed as she refilled his meadar with buttermilk.

After we had eaten I told my family that I would be visiting Teige for a week or more and mounting the garron set off with Rory. Early the following morning Teige and Rory on saddle horses and I on the garron rode east towards Leitrim. We had shaggy mantles in which we could wrap ourselves at night, enough cakes and ale to last us for three or four days and Teige and Rory were armed with sharp-edged miodoges and pistols.

Before we reached the Shannon half a dozen armed horsemen appeared on the road ahead. At once we raced uphill towards a nearby wood but before we gained its shelter, pistol balls whizzed past us. I heard Teige cry out then we were dismounting and tying the horses to trees. Teige had been hit in the left shoulder so while Rory frantically primed the two pistols and lit spunk using a flint and steel I tried to staunch and bandage the wound. By now the horsemen, probably fearing an ambush, had dismounted also and, walking about twelve paces apart, were advancing cautiously uphill.

Just as I finished tying a strip of his shirt around Teige's shoulder Rory finally got the slow matches of both pistols burning. Closing one eye I peeped past a tree and recognised the tallest of our attackers: it was Young Sir Charles Coote.

"Throw a stone at them then duck!" Rory hissed.

I did as he instructed, whereupon about four shots rang out and pistol balls struck the tree trunks beside us. Rory quickly discharged a pistol then taking careful aim discharged the other one. His ball must have struck home because there was a yell of pain followed by more shots. When I peeped out our attackers were withdrawing, two of them carrying a wounded man, the others, including Coote, casting occasional backwards glances till they reached the horses.

"If only we had the wheel-lock pistols those mongrels have, I could charge them now," Rory lamented.

Gambling that the horsemen were tending to their comrade, we slipped quietly out the other side of the wood. Teige was in great pain, forcing us to ride slowly. Every minute we expected to hear the sound of pursuit but none came. After travelling east for an hour we crossed the Shannon at Battle Bridge then brought Teige to the home of the local chieftain, an O'Rourke, where we were made welcome.

In no time a healer arrived to examine Teige's shoulder. Probing and gouging with a heated knife, this mild-mannered fellow eventually removed the pistol ball. He told Teige that because the ball had come close to a heart vein he would have to rest there till the wound mended. On hearing this Teige, who was still pale from his ordeal, beckoned me over to his pallet.

"Daibhí," he said, "this changes everything. I can't let you go to Ulster."

"But I want to go," I protested.

"Listen!" He grasped my wrist with his right hand, the other being strapped to his chest: "Our family dismissed you after the feast so that frees you from any obligation. Rory can get two of the O'Rourkes to take our place. You've a lame leg and God alone knows what's lying in wait up north. This wound of mine may be just a foretaste."

"All the same, I'm going," I assured him. "Now tell me what you found out about Úna."

Convinced that my mind was made up, he whispered that a Franciscan friar had seen a woman with long fair hair who was dressed as a man lying sick in Cloghoughter Castle. This castle was now in the hands of the O'Reillys, who had garrisoned it. The friar had brought news of the woman to Cavan town, from where it had been passed along by other friars till it reached the ears of Bishop Egan, himself a Franciscan. It was Bishop Egan who had informed Turlough. If I succeeded in getting Úna safely out of East Breifne I was to bring her to his house in Oughtertire. On no account was I to reveal her whereabouts to anybody other than Turlough. Finally, he told me to take his saddle horse for Úna as well as the garron.

We spent what remained of the evening discussing the uprising in Ulster with the O'Rourke family and talking about their kinsman, Brian Oge, who had fought at the Battle of the Curlews. Next morning, mounted on Teige's horse, and with the garron on a lead, I rode after Rory towards Cavan. We made good progress, sleeping that night on rushes in the cabin of a friendly herdsman. The following day was wet, causing us much discomfort. By nightfall we were obliged to lie down on brushwood in a small grove, using our mantles for cover. In the morning I felt stiff and miserable and my bad leg ached.

Thereafter as we got further east, skirting loughs and marshes, we often slept in woods since people would not give us shelter, the uprising having made them distrustful of strangers.

Eventually, having passed a number of burnt-out houses, we arrived tired and weary at the mansion of the Protestant Bishop, Doctor Bedell, which was filled with English planters who had been driven from their homes. This good man, lamenting that he could not offer us hospitality, directed us to Cloghoughter Castle, a few miles away to the northwest in Lough Oughter.

After taking many wrong turns among trees fringing the twisting fingers of water which border the lough we heard people chanting, "*An lile ba léir é, ba linn an lá*" – The lily was plain to see, the day was ours – and heading in that direction ran into a band of jubilant rebels, armed with pikes, sickles and hatchets, some of them wearing clothes stripped from the planters. Once they had assured themselves that we were Gaels they led us to the shore opposite the castle. Bidding us wait there, three of them rowed across to the island fortress and presently returned with the governor, Owen O'Reilly, a harassed-looking man of middle years armed with a sword and wearing a steel breastplate. When he had learned the nature of our quest, O'Reilly shook his head.

"She's not here," he told us. "She's with the canons below in Trinity Island. I had to send her there for her own safety – This castle is for prisoners, some of them quite desperate. I'll have two of my *kernes* escort you to the monastery."

Thanking O'Reilly for his help we set off, the barefooted *kernes* armed with pikes easily keeping pace with our horses. Before we reached the vicinity of the island, Rory halted. When I asked him why, he said: "This is as far as I go. My home is a half day's ride over there, in Aghanure – though the Planters call it Virginia."

"Why can't you wait till tomorrow?" I protested.

He shook his head: "For the past twelve years I've dreamt of setting eyes on that spot. Now with the place so near, every minute's delay seems a lifetime."

118

Since he had been my guide and protector on the long dangerous journey I bade him farewell with a heavy heart. A few minutes later I was being rowed in a currach to the island by one of the kernes, while his fellow remained behind to guard the horses. A monk dressed in white robes, who might have stepped out of the picture flanking the shrine in MacDermots' castle, greeted me warmly and led me past mud and wattle huts into a freshly thatched house near a roofless stone church with a tall belfry. In the dim interior of the house I saw an old woman bending over somebody propped up on a pallet. She was feeding the person from a wooden bowl with a spoon. When my eyes became adjusted to the gloom my heart almost stopped beating so painful was my joy on recognising the long fair hair.

"Úna," I cried, "it's me."

She looked at me dully then in a weak voice said, "What brings you here?"

Chapter 24

Despite my disappointment and tiredness I resolved to be cheerful. When I had told Úna the reason for my visit, the old woman said she would return later to give Úna the rest of her herbal gruel and shuffled out. Now that we were alone Úna lay down and turned her face to the wall as if to sleep.

"Listen," I decided to plunge in, "there's another reason why I came. Before the feast Honora, may her soul be at God's right hand, gave me a letter your father wrote to you."

On hearing this she tuned to face me. "Is Honora dead then?"

"Yes," I replied. "She passed away the night you disappeared. When your family couldn't find any trace of you they were frantic, thinking you must have drowned yourself."

"Am I supposed to feel guilty because of that?" She sat up. "I'm sorry Honora died but she never liked me. Why else would she keep a letter my father wrote to me? Anyway, where's the letter now?"

I confessed that I hadn't brought it with me, believing it would be best to keep it till she was safely back in Moylurg. When she accused me of trying to trick her into returning I recounted all I had done to find her, even to giving Kevin my own letter in Sligo. She listened quietly then said she was sorry for being ungrateful.

"You must think me heartless," she added, "but I've seen such horrible sights, things that ... I was in Fermanagh with Manus. At first we were... we were taking back what had been stolen from our people...then the men began drinking *usquebagh*. I begged Manus to stop them but he told me their day had come, that it was now the Planters turn to be treated like wild beasts, the way they had treated us... I saw men hacked to death before their wives and children – They even ran one woman through with a sword because she tried to shield her husband. What's dying of an illness compared to that? Honora was fortunate, yes she really was. In one place I saw women, after their men had been butchered, stripped of their clothes and left to walk barefooted and naked with their children on the road to Dublin. Another time Manus ordered his *kernes* to lock men, women and children into a barn and then set the place on fire. I told him that if he didn't stop I was leaving but he was too drunk to listen...He said they were English dogs – And to think I trusted him... "

"Is that when you did leave?" I prompted when she seemed too distraught to continue.

"No," she whispered, "I tried to walk away but it was pitch black – I don't want to talk about it anymore. It's a nightmare I want to put out of my head. Owen O'Reilly has been good to me, as have the monks here – Do you know they're not supposed to have women on the island but Owen told them that if they didn't take me, and that herb woman, I'd probably die. He also promised to put a roof on their church. This will be the new refectory... I like it here... It's the first time in years that I've felt at peace. If I were a man I think I'd join the White Canons..."

Seeing that she was becoming drowsy, I told her to sleep and, promising to be there when she awoke, tiptoed away. The old woman took me to the abbot, Father Cillian, in another thatched house further back. He asked me who Úna was and on obtaining his promise that he would not reveal it to anybody I told him.

"Isn't that an example of God's providence?" he remarked. "It was Canons from Trinity Island in Lough Key who founded this monastery and now a daughter of the family that endowed and protected them in Moylurg finds refuge here."

After we had discussed the MacDermots and my own kinsmen in Castlefore, of whose piety and learning he had often heard, he invited me to stay with them till Úna had recovered. When I agreed, he instructed the kerne to take the currach to the opposite shore and get his comrade to swim the horses across. This the man promptly did so that in half an hour my dripping garron and the saddle horse were safely on the island, where there was a large pasture sheltered by oak trees.

During the following days I often sat beside Úna's pallet, sometimes feeding her the herbal gruel, which she disliked, at other times listening to her accounts of the rising in Fermanagh. She told me Brian Maguire had informed the New Gall about their plans to take Enniskillen Castle and it was because of this that Lord Conor Maguire, one of their principal leaders, had been captured in Dublin. The rising had gone ahead without him so that now the planters were under siege in a few fortified towns and castles. She herself had taken part in attacks, carrying a banner and encouraging the fighters; she hadn't killed anybody. Where the leaders were at hand they wouldn't allow any massacres – some of them had even threatened to hang those who mistreated prisoners. But demons like Manus were out for vengeance.

Finally I learned about her flight. She had joined an English woman Manus and his men had stripped, determined to protect her and her children on their walk towards Cavan. She had given the woman her cloak even though she herself was cold. Nobody along the way would help them. They had to sleep under bushes, sometimes within a stone's throw of Lough Erne. Often they were in danger from bands of rebels but because she was able to convince them that Manus had ordered her to insure the family's safety she had saved them from further harm. Nevertheless the youngest children soon weakened.

On reaching Belturbet they were afraid of being challenged by vengeful O'Reilly kernes if they tried to cross the bridge so they had forded the Erne. Unfortunately, two of the children had slipped and fallen into the water. Their clothes were soaking, adding to their distress. She herself had carried the baby across safely, then, because it was dying, she had walked up to a cabin with the tiny creature in her arms and the smaller children at her side. The woman of the house had taken pity on them and given her bread and milk. But it was too late for the baby and her little brother. The bread didn't last long and by the time they trudged into Cavan hungry and exhausted another child had died.

People brought them to the sheriff, a brother of the O'Reilly chieftain.

She didn't know what happened next because she had collapsed. When she came to she was lying on a pallet in Cloghoughter Castle, burning up with fever. The governor, Owen O'Reilly, had kept her in his own room for safety. He told her later that he had sent the mother and her three remaining children to Bishop Bedell's house. She couldn't be sure how many weeks she had lain near death because the fever waxed and waned. At times she thought she was back in her own room in Carrick Mansion, at other times that she was holding the dead infant, trying to bring it back to life. It could have been her own child...

"The child you lost after the feast?" The words were out before I realised it.

She flared up. "Who told you that?"

I recounted what I had heard the Virgin say when I was praying at the shrine.

"It's true," she admitted. "I took *gafann* to make me sleep. That night my baby was stillborn. I suppose you'll despise me now like all the others?"

I assured her that I wouldn't and asked how Thomas had felt.

"He didn't know," she replied, "and even if he did I wouldn't care, not after his refusal to come back when he was sent for. His pride was more important than my suffering."

"You know he thinks you're dead?" I remarked and told her about the song I had heard the *geocach* singing in Sligo.

"I am dead," she replied. "I died a long time ago, even before I met Thomas. That's why I want to remain here forever."

On saying this she closed her eyes and, sick at heart, I tiptoed out.

Chapter 25

The first sign that Úna was better was a wish she expressed to repay the monks for their hospitality – I'm calling them monks because that's what Úna called them, though they left the island daily to minister to the people.

"Why don't you paint another picture of the Annunciation?" I suggested.

Immediately her eyes grew bright. "I know what," she said, "I'll paint the *Miracle of the Loaves and Fishes* on that wall. Ask them for paints and brushes."

When I told Father Cillian of her offer, citing her skill as an artist, he readily gave his assent.

"Once we had the most beautiful church in Cavan," he declared, "but first the stone doorway was taken and then the roof destroyed. I'll find the paints somehow – we have white and the friars in the town may have some saffron and umber; I'll get indigo and rose, even if we have to beg them from Doctor Bedell – I did send him a bushel of oatmeal last week to help feed those poor, homeless people he's sheltering. Anyway, I'll move heaven and earth and if the mural turns out well, we'll get Úna to do a triptych for the altar."

He was as good as his word, so that a few days later Úna was painting Jesus, using as her model Brother Colm, the first monk I had encountered on entering the island. Every few hours some monk would tiptoe in to wonder at the scene coming to life on the plastered wall, while Úna, paint all over her hands and cheeks, would try to hide her annoyance. She was using me as a model for one of the disciples when another monk distracted her, causing her hand to slip. Immediately she became distressed, claiming the painting was now ruined. It was with difficulty that I persuaded her not to deface the entire scene but she refused to work on it again.

Deciding that the time to leave had come, I broached the subject to Úna and with a nervous look in her eyes she agreed. Father Cillian gave her a cloak as well as provisions for our journey and assured her that, even though incomplete, her mural was beautiful: Jesus with his saffron robe, blue cloak and mild, radiant countenance was the equal of anything he had ever laid eyes on.

"Your picture is like our task of repairing what that apostate Henry the Eighth destroyed," he observed, "half finished, but as the proverb has it 'A good start is half the work.'"

There is one episode in our journey west that stands out above all others. On a cold, wet day near Carrigallen we came upon a half-naked young woman with two small, hollow-cheeked children, their hands out, begging wordlessly. Without a thought for her-own health, Úna removed Father Cillian's cloak and handed it to the woman. Ignoring her protests, I retrieved the cloak and gave the woman some of our provisions. When Úna berated me for my lack of charity, I reminded her that I had promised Teige to bring her back alive.

"What does my life matter?" she responded. "Her need is greater than mine."

On many occasions after that I saw Úna's compassion for the poor and wretched, as if her experiences in Fermanagh had pierced her heart.

Christmas had come and gone by the time we approached the Shannon, having spent two days with my kinsmen in Castlefore and another with the O'Rourke family to allow Úna to rest. O'Rourke's wife told us that her husband was away with the North Connacht chieftains near Sligo and that Teige had been seen with his cousin, Owen MacDermot of Drumdoe, during the recent siege of the town. There were rumours that a number of Protestants who had sought refuge in Sligo jail had been killed by a drunken mob but she didn't know how many.

Next day we crossed the Shannon. The closer we got to Oughtertire the more agitated Úna became so that finally I prevailed on her to come with me to our house. My mother and Eileen greeted us both like long lost children, having given me up for dead. Even Philip welcomed us, though he had been without the garron for weeks.

"I'll ask Teige to give you one of his," Úna promised, which made Philip remark that Teige could give a garron to me; he would be content with his own.

Eileen was worried that Rory might be killed in East Breifne but I told her that places like Aghanure were safe, the planters having been driven into two castles near Killeshandra. That night Eileen gave Úna her pallet while she herself slept with my mother in the bed. Next morning, having eaten a bowl of oatmeal porridge and some griddlecake, Úna suddenly announced that she was going to Sligo to find Teige. Since she couldn't be dissuaded I was obliged to borrow Philip's garron once more and, despite my misgivings, set out with her.

We made good progress and found lodgings that night in the MacDonagh castle in Collooney. Úna in her doublet and breeches excited much curiosity but I convinced people that she was my cousin, Úna O'Reilly from Cavan, who had dressed like this to avoid the attention of soldiers. MacDonagh wasn't there, he having taken the field weeks previously with O'Connor Sligo, Plunkett, O'Rourke, MacBrian, Taaffe, O'Dowd and other insurgents.

Next day we entered Sligo, which was like a bees' nest that has been robbed: furniture piled outside burned houses; a tattered Saint George banner being dragged along by urchins; green cloths hanging from upstairs windows; bands of armed soldiers issuing unexpectedly out of alleys or marching down the filth-strewn streets; wild-looking kernes singing with drunken bravado; men driving carts with bound hogs and a few townswomen hurrying here and there as if anxious to be indoors. Nobody challenged us as we rode slowly towards the half-empty market square. I still had the pistol Teige had given me but it was unloaded – Úna with the *miodogue* in a leather scabbard hanging from her belt presented a more warlike demeanour.

A soldier armed with a matchlock musket told us that Teige and Owen were probably with the commander-in-chief, Brian MacDonagh of Tirerrill, over at the main "castle". On approaching this strong-house, which had a banner showing a diagonal red cross on a white field flying from its battlements, we were denied entry by the guards until, feigning impatience, I informed them that we had just come from the fighting in Ulster. On hearing this one of them conducted us to the hall where MacDonagh, a fresh-faced young man, was drinking *usquebagh* at a table with his lieutenants. When I had given them my name and repeated the story of Úna being my cousin, MacDonagh welcomed us courteously, remarking that he had often heard his father praise my family. He then listened with rapt attention to Úna's account of the rising in Fermanagh.

"If only our men were as brave as you," he smiled at Úna, "we'd soon drive the New Gall back to England. As for finding Teige and Owen MacDermot, they're conducting prisoners to the English garrison in Abbeyboyle – it's part of the terms we agreed to at their surrender. Will you go after them – I can give you an escort – or will you wait here till they return?"

Úna told him we would wait, offering, if he let us stay in the "castle", to make him a new banner since the one he had, which he called a Saint Patrick Cross, was too like the Cross of Saint George.

"It'll be a golden sun rising above a green hill to show our day has come," she explained, her eyes gleaming.

"I had in mind a gold harp on a green field myself." He rubbed his chin for a moment then looked me directly in the eye. "Daibhí, you come from a family of scholars. What do you think?"

"Una is a true artist." I tried to conceal my pride at his question. "You should see the *Miracle of the Loaves and Fishes* she painted for the White Canons above in Cavan, so we can't go far wrong if we trust in her judgment – And wasn't Finn MacCumhail's banner said to be a blazing sun?"

"In that case," he made up his mind on the instant, "the rising sun it'll be. We're going to have a new day in Ireland just as we always hoped – that's if the rest of the country joins us before the New Gall are ready."

The strong-house being overcrowded, he assigned us a garret in "Jones's Castle" nearby, a tiny room that was used to store pails and besoms. The only light came from a broken hole in the roof.

After examining the bed of rushes covered with a pair of coarse *bréidín* blankets which one of MacDonagh's kernes had prepared for us, Úna began to unfasten her doublet.

"Turn your back!" she commanded as I stood watching openmouthed.

When she had slipped between the blankets, over which we had spread our mantles, she told me I could undress. Hardly daring to believe my ears I hastily stripped to my shirt and got in beside her. Since we were both cold she allowed me to hold her in my arms. Immediately I found she was still in the shift worn under her doublet but this light garment only enhanced the soft roundness of her body, which gave off a rich, sweetish odour like newly-baked griddle cake.

As though I were in paradise I listened to her recount how she had fallen in love with Costello. He was the first man to whom she had given her heart but when she found she was with child she was panicstricken.

"I knew after he struck me at the feast that Cathal Roe would never consent to my marrying Thomas so I took the *gafann* to get rid of ... of the child growing in my womb," she mumbled, adding in a dejected voice, "You'll hardly think me a sunbeam now."

"What's done is done," I said, my right hand moving in wonder down the deep curve of her hip to her waist. "You told me you couldn't sleep that night and your mind was clouded with pain and despair. God won't judge you as harshly as you judge yourself."

"I knew you'd say that!" she retorted. "How can a man know what a woman feels?"

Instead of answering, I cupped her breast in my hand, intoxicated by its yielding suppleness. For a while she suffered my caress, then sitting up abruptly, ordered me out of the bed.

129

Reluctantly I got up, my mind screaming that this was how Adam felt on being expelled from Paradise. Why hadn't I been content to lie quietly beside her?

"We'll have to sleep head to toe," she decided.

Knowing there would be no good in pleading, I reluctantly complied. So it was that Úna and I shared the same bed, though we might have been brother and sister for all the good it did me. Still, we were closer than we had been before arriving in Sligo and I was able to warn away a drunken soldier who banged on our door in the darkness, demanding to be let in.

The very next day we called to the house of the Lutheran minister, Reverend Newport, now taken over by a widow and her family. This good woman found saffron and green gowns in a cupboard and Úna, using a white sheet for the sky, cut out the different pieces, which the widow sewed together into a banner. It was my task to get the pike handle to which they attached it. A crowd of barefooted urchins marched behind us back to the main "castle" as Úna carried the rising sun fluttering proudly above her head. Once we were back in this strong-house MacDonagh pronounced the banner magnificent and directed a soldier to hang it from the battlements. If only such bright days might last.

Chapter 26

Before we retired that night Úna suddenly demanded her father's letter. I had been reluctant to remind her of it, fearing that it would only open old wounds, but she was not to be denied. She read the contents by the light of our rush candle then wordlessly held the paper sheets to the flame.

"Why are you doing that?" I exclaimed.

"Do you think I want to listen to his excuses?" She spoke in a dead voice. "If he were a true father do you think he'd be ready to barter me for the family's safety?"

"It struck me as a loving letter," I demurred.

"Yes," she agreed. "Father – no, Dada could use honeyed words. Do you know who's holding Abbeyboyle for the New Gall? Sir Robert King, the man whose son he wanted me to marry. If I were Turlough I'd have stormed the abbey – which is rightfully ours – and his halfbuilt castle by now."

"But I thought that after Fermanagh you'd have enough of fighting?"

"I won't have enough till we have justice," she said. "In Ulster people's land was given to foreigners who despised their Gaelic ways and plundered their churches. Down here our priests are outlawed and our land is also going to be planted. I'm not defending what Manus did, burning and killing, but the chieftains don't want that. You heard MacDonagh say how he allowed the garrison here safe passage to Abbeyboyle. Would the New Gall be so generous if ever they defeated us?"

"They're better armed and have stronger castles so, unless we get help from Spain or France, maybe they will defeat us," I told her.

"Oh, you're too timid," she scoffed. "When Teige comes back, I'm going to ask him to take me to Ballintober. We'll have Hugh O'Conor proclaimed king on Carnfree and then, just as Saint Bearchán foretold, victory will be ours!"

Listening to her with her eyes shining and her old enthusiasm rekindled I could almost believe that this time, despite the number of chieftains who were holding back or siding with the New Gall, we would be victorious. That night, however, I heard her whimpering, "Dada! Dada! Take me with you! Don't leave me, Dada!" and it chilled my blood, as if she were addressing a ghost.

It was a week before Teige returned, having first visited Carrick Mansion and Cloonybrien. He was overjoyed to see Úna safe, being certain she was dead or captured. Úna recounted her experiences in Ulster and warned him not to tell anyone who she was. He said that their cousin Owen was still back at Drumdoe.

"What did Turlough say about the rising?" Úna asked impatiently.

Teige told her that Turlough had been among the Roscommon chieftains who had met in Ballintober at Christmas and had taken an oath to support King Charles and maintain the Catholic faith. There was fierce fighting in that part of the county, the insurgents having burnt Elphin and, with Con O'Rourke leading them, attacked Roscommon. Now Con O'Rourke and Hugh O'Conor at the head of twelve hundred men were going to besiege Castlecoote, the stronghold of Young Sir Charles Coote, the very devil who had tried to kill him.

On hearing this Úna decided she and Teige should set out at once for Ballintober. She was tired of doing nothing in Sligo except making banners. Teige tried to dissuade her, saying he had promised Turlough to help him raise a regiment in Moylurg. Sir Robert King had already raised a troop of Horse, which his son John had used to relieve Elphin.

"If you won't come with me then Daibhí will," Úna declared.

"But Daibhí has a lame leg," Teige objected. "You can't expect him to fight."

"He brought me back from Cavan," Úna pointed out. "You will come with me, won't you, Daibhí?"

"Why don't we first see what we can do here?" I countered, having no desire to rush blindly into trouble. "You heard Owen Mór O'Rourke warn the other day he believes that

132

Sir Frederick Hamilton is getting ready to attack Sligo. And, anyway, I will have to give Philip back his garron."

"Owen Mór is always going on about Hamilton!" Úna tossed her head. "As for the garron, Teige will give you one of his – Won't you, Teige?"

The end of the discussion was that rather than let her venture out on her own I agreed to go with Úna. Teige too reluctantly yielded, promising me a garron belonging to one of his men. While Úna was out in the garderobe he took a handful of shillings from his girdle, entreating me to insure that his sister didn't go hungry and not to let her risk her life or let myself be swayed by her judgments of others.

"With Úna it's always been everything or nothing," he confided. "If she can't be first in somebody's affections she casts him off."

"Is that why she turned against your father?" I asked.

Teige looked thoughtful. "It could be," he said. "She resented our sisters and, above all, mother – I suppose she's fond of Turlough and myself, though I..."

Úna's return caused him to leave the rest unsaid.

Before setting out we packed a banner in one of the saddlebags then, on thanking MacDonagh for his kindness, I warned him about Hamilton.

" Leave Sir Frederick to us." The commander smiled. "We'll drive him and his mongrels back to Manorhamilton with their tails between their legs."

"By the way," I said, "that mountain that looks like an upturned currach, the one you can see just north of here, what's it called?"

"Shouldn't a scholar like you be telling me?" He shook his head in mock reproof. "That's Benbulben, where Diarmuid O'Duibhne was killed by the wild boar. If you go down to the cabins by the river, there's a shanachie, Blind Ciaran, who'll tell you all about it.

"You're not going to waste time looking for that man?" Úna protested after we had taken leave of MacDonagh. "It's almost noontide now."

"It won't take long." Ignoring her frown, I mounted my garron and taking the reins of Teige's garron, trotted back past the gaol, where the recent slaughter had taken place, to a laneway leading to the Garavogue. She followed slowly on her horse.

Having made enquiries in a windowless cabin, I was told Ciaran was out fishing. In a little while we came upon him, a ragged greybeard sitting on an upturned creel, smoking a pipe while his grown-up son cast out a fish net.

Úna refused to dismount, reminding me that I had promised to take her to Ballintober and adding that the war against the New Gall was surely more important than a story about some longago boar hunt.

"It would be foolish not to hear his version," I managed to hide my annoyance that despite all I had undertaken for her sake she thought so little of my work.

"Couldn't you wait till your next visit?" she grumbled but, having a foreboding that one or both of us would never again set foot in Sligo, I didn't answer.

Blind Ciaran turned out to be the best shanachie I had yet encountered. He also had an account of *The Pursuit of Diarmuid and Grainne* which I had never heard before, that Finn MacCumhail had taken the shape of the boar in order to kill his rival; nevertheless, while he chanted I was distracted by the sight of Úna glowering on her horse as she held the reins of Teige's and my garron. At last, fearing that she might ride off without me, I paid Ciaran a shilling and regretfully bade him farewell.

"Can we waste no more time?" Úna begged when I had remounted.

"That wasn't a waste of time," I refused to humour her mood. "It's stories like *The Pursuit* which kept people's spirits up through centuries of invasion and pillage."

"Now's the time for fighting, not for listening to shanachies," she retorted.

As we were approaching the market square we could hear the *geocach* singing to a rapt crowd of *scullogues*, townspeople and soldiers:

> *"The Erne shall gather in torrents and hills shall be rent,*
> *The waves of the sea shall redden and blood will be spilt,*
> *Every mountain glen and bog in Ireland shall quake*
> *One day before my Little Black Rose will die."*

"Wasn't it Thomas's father who composed that?" I remarked without thinking.

Instead of answering, Úna dug her heels into her horse's flanks and I tried to keep up, with Teige's riderless garron cantering beside me. Why in heaven's name hadn't I realised that any mention of Thomas would open a wound that was still raw? On passing the house before which the New Gall sentry had stood, I could see her banner flying above it, then I was turning south through burned cabins towards Collooney. By this time Úna was far ahead and, loath to endure her abandonment of reason – for so, from lingering pique, I judged it – I slowed to a trot. Gradually she passed out of sight. However, I told myself that she would soon come to her senses but an hour later there was still no sign of her.

The fear that she might have been waylaid gradually took hold of me. What was I to do? If I pushed the garrons to a faster pace they would only become winded. With mounting unease I pressed ahead, mile after mile, scanning the deserted fields flanked by gloomy woods. The weather was mild for February with only passing showers of rain. Suddenly I noticed smoke rising from a group of smouldering cabins. When I rode up nobody answered my halloos. A sickly-sweet smell hung in the air. Within a fire-blackened ruin I found the burnt corpses of men, women and children. Nauseous I hurried away. If Úna had come upon this village why hadn't she stopped?

I was almost giving up hope of finding her when I spied her hat lying by the road edge. Further on I came upon her doublet, shift and breeches scattered here and there. My blood ran cold. Praying that she hadn't been killed, I flailed the garron into a canter. Then I saw her, naked as Eve, half crouched, shivering under a holly bush, her white body smeared with grime and blood, her long hair covering her face.

"Who did it?" I shouted, dismounting.

She didn't answer nor even raise her head.

Chapter 27

Placing my mantle around Úna I left her and rode back to gather up her clothes. It struck me that if her attackers had been woodkernes they would not have thrown away such valuable garments. Hurrying back, I found her again half crouched and had to persuade her to dress quickly before she caught an ague. When she still wouldn't talk I helped her onto Teige's garron, her own horse having been taken, and clasping her tightly about the waist rode with her till we came to a stone cattle barn beside a roofless, burnt-out mansion. Here using my flint and steel I made a fire from dry cattle dung and sticks from a jackdaw's nest and placing her on a pile of branches before it coaxed her to eat some of our bread. At last she took a few mouthfuls then lay down with her head resting on a saddlebag and closed her eyes. I stayed awake as long I could, feeding the fire with branches and stroking her hair. She moaned and trembled but finally sank into a deeper sleep.

Next day I tried to get Úna to speak but she just hung her head or looked at me with empty eyes. Cursing myself for my thoughtless mention of Thomas, as well as the delay caused by talking to Blind Ciaran, I resolved not to let her out of my sight again. After eating some more of our bread, I helped her on to Teige's garron. The weather promised fair so we set off for Kilmactranny, bypassing Collooney in the hope of reaching home before sunset. With a few stops to rest the garrons and eat, we rode in the well-known boreen just as darkness was falling.

My mother and Eileen fussed over Úna as if she was their own child. They coaxed her into eating a bowl of hot gruel before telling Philip and me to go outside while they washed her and put her to bed. As we walked down the boreen by the light of the rising moon Philip asked me about the fighting in Sligo. He was pleased to hear that it was the Tirerrill chieftain, Brian MacDonagh, who was in charge. Having asked if Úna and I were going to marry he revealed that he himself was betrothed to a girl from the other end of the parish, a Deirdre MacDonagh.

"If you get Úna to accept you, we can both be connected to great Gaelic families," he said. "And why shouldn't we? Aren't the O'Duigenans their equal?"

For almost a fortnight my mother and Eileen took care of Úna, killing a hen to make broth, washing her clothes and sending me for the healer. Gradually she lost her dazed look and when Philip and I were outside she spoke to them, brokenly at first then in a flood of bitter words. Eileen, reluctant to repeat what had been told in confidence, would only hint at what had happened, so I will set down here Úna's own account from a letter penned to her brother about two months later – It was during a visit to Coolavin last year that Teige showed me part of the letter, saying that if I intended to write about his sister it was best that my account be truthful. Here then is what Úna wrote:

When we left Sligo I was furious with Daibhí. For all his learning he's just like other men, convinced that women are empty-headed creatures fit only to mind the house and raise children. He even tried to embrace me – though I was partly to blame. Anyway, he thinks we should be wary of attacking the New Gall, as if the time for hesitation hadn't long passed. Now that the country is ablaze only the strong will withstand the flames. Joan of Arc found the Dauphin afraid to fight, so she herself led the French army at Orleans and though, in the end, she was burned at the stake, the English were driven out of France. I hope that I'll have the same resolve – but I'm getting away from that awful day in Sligo.

When we were riding out of the town a geocach was singing 'Róisín Dubh' and, as if that weren't bad enough, Daibhí had to remind me that it was Thomas's father who made it, probably to pay me back for not having accepted him. Well, I was determined to have nothing more to do with our too-clever scribe so I galloped ahead till he was out of sight, not a very difficult feat since he moves so slowly at whatever he does, weighing this course and that like a miller weighing corn. After some time I slowed to a trot so that the horse wouldn't get winded. By now I was resolved to spend the night in Collooney Castle, then ride next day to Oughtertire and stay with you – If darkness overtook me on the road to Oughtertire I would ask for shelter in some cabin. Well over an hour passed without my encountering anybody, something that should have put me on my guard. Eventually I saw smoke billowing up in the distance and, without hesitation, rode forward till I came to a wrecked village.

What a shock that was! The smell of burning timber and rushes mingled with the odour of roasting flesh brought me back again to Fermanagh on the evening when Manus persuaded his kinsman, Rory Maguire, to burn the poor, frightened men, women and children they had locked inside a barn. I recalled pleading with them to stop but they were so filled with usquebagh and hatred they just swore at me. Now the memory of that awful time made me unable to search the smoldering cabins for anybody who might still be alive, so I just shouted over and over, "Is there anybody here?" That was my undoing.

Suddenly half a dozen men mounted on strong horses and armed with swords and pistols galloped up, encircling me. Seeing from their clothes that they were New Gall, I addressed them in English, asking what had happened to the village. Their leader, a pockmarked villain with cold eyes and thin, cruel lips partly covered by a fawn moustache, informed me that the Romish rats had been burned alive as a warning to other rebels.

"Who are you and what brings you here?" he then demanded.

"I'm Mistress Sinclair, wife of Isaac Sinclair, verger in Sligo church," I lied. "I'm on my way to Abbeyboyle to join my husband. He was sent there under escort by Brian MacDonagh, the rebel commander."

"And why are you travelling alone, Mistress Sinclair?" a long-faced fellow with crooked yellow teeth sneered.

"Two of MacDonagh's men were escorting me, but fearing they meant me harm, I eluded them a while back," I told him, sweat starting to break out on my forehead.

"Who is minister in Sligo church?" A tall, well-spoken youth asked.

"Reverend Newport," I told him. "He went with the others to Abbeyboyle."

"What is Reverend Newport's Christian name?" Pockface broke in and when I hesitated, he continued, "Since when does an honest verger's wife speak Gaelic and wear men's clothes?"

Knowing by his voice that he was growing tired of playing cat-and-mouse with me, I dug my heels into the horse's flanks, broke through the circle of leering devils and galloped away. It was a doomed attempt. Before I had gone a hundred paces they caught up with me. One of them grabbed my reins. Another lifted me from the horse's back and dropped me to the ground.

"Strip the papist witch!" Pockface ordered as they all dismounted.

I screamed and struggled but one by one they tore off my garments, allowing me to escape then quickly overtaking me. All this time I was telling myself that somebody would hear my screams but, probably fearing the same thing, a red-faced bodach slapped me across the mouth till I almost fainted. After that they had their way with me, swearing and jeering like demons out of hell. While it was happening I made myself think of Joan standing bound to the stake as flames devoured her limbs and body. Again and again pain seared through me till I longed for death. As if in answer to my wish Pockface said to the long-faced fellow, "Cut her throat."

"No!" the tall youth protested, half drawing his sword. "We musn't blacken our souls any further."

"Have it your own way," Pockface remarked, "but, upon my soul, the papist witch will only breed more rebels."

With that the hellhounds, who might have been Hamilton's men, rode away, leaving me broken and degraded. My mind and body were so numb that I scarcely knew if I was still alive. It was in that state that Daibhí found me. I remember wishing he would not call my soul back from the dark country in which it hovered, back to where it could feel again the pain in my

140

loins and the taste of blood in my mouth. His gentleness, however, melted any anger I harboured against him, and, indeed, were it not for his help and the solicitude of his family I should never have come alive out of Sligo. I'm telling you all this so that you'll understand why I cannot rest till our people have thrown off their oppressors, for even as I write the leering faces and stinking breaths of my attackers almost overwhelms me.

After what had befallen Úna I now believed she would consent to return to her family. Why should she risk the same thing happening again? Perhaps it was a desire for revenge on the New Gall or just a determination to fulfil what she saw as her destiny but when I mentioned Carrick Mansion she told me in a quiet voice she was going to Ballintober. Nothing I said would weaken her resolve so one bleak morning, my mind filled with foreboding, I rode off with her. Phillip had again given me the garron, declaring that it was the least he could do for his country and faith.

"Drive the foreign devils out of Ireland!" he shouted after us.

Snow was falling by the time we crossed the Boyle River at Knockvicar. I wanted to turn back but Úna rode doggedly on. By the time we reached Ardcarn the snow was so thick that we had to seek shelter from the old couple who had helped me before. They were amazed to see Úna, whom they remembered from her visits to the village with Manus but had since been told was dead. When they recovered from their surprise they fussed over her because she looked so tired and wan. In truth she had lost much of her former brightness, her hair, which was now almost flaxen, mirroring the pallor of her gaunt cheeks. She told them she had fallen ill in Cavan but begged them never to tell anyone they had seen her as Manus had vowed to kill her for deserting him.

We slept that night on piles of rushes by the smoke-darkened wall, our hosts stretched out side by side beyond us. Having eaten next morning and offered the kindly couple payment, which they indignantly refused, we rode off before the village was astir. The snow had stopped so that we made good progress, reaching Croghan about midday. Though we saw chimney smoke from the O'Mulloys' stronghouse rising from the woods, Úna would not hear of calling on them, knowing that they would report her whereabouts to Carrick Mansion.

After a pause to eat we continued our journey, staying that night in a cabin near Elphin. The town had been burned but the Red Cross banner of Saint George still flew defiantly over the bishop's fortified palace. The people gathered in the house told us Hugh O'Conor and Con O'Rourke had besieged the palace for three or four days but the arrival of a troop of Horse from Abbeyboyle had forced them to withdraw. Úna was delighted to hear that Hugh was in the forefront of the fighting, telling our hosts that Saint Bearchán had foretold that he would free Ireland, a story that caused great excitement until one greybeard asked, "Wasn't the Hugh in the prophesy supposed to be red-handed?"

"And isn't Hugh's hand now red with the blood of our enemies?" Úna replied, to which the greybeard could only respond that he supposed so.

During this discussion I noted in Úna a hardness that wasn't there before. She brushed aside any talk of compassion for New Gall who had acquired lands, whether by royal grant, mortgage or purchase, since the Composition of Connacht, lamenting only that we hadn't muskets and cannon to match theirs. Bishop Tilson, the Lutheran from Dublin whose palace Hugh O'Conor had attacked, had filched the palace from our Bishop Egan, who was obliged to sneak around disguised as a merchant. The people listened to this fiery young woman in doublet and breeches as if she were the war goddess Macha come back to rouse them from their lethargy. They then told her about a widow living nearby whose only son had been wounded in the siege and nothing would satisfy Úna but that we should visit them.

When we entered the pungent, smoky cabin, Úna was so moved by the sight of the young man, his head bound in bloodstained cloths, lying on a pile of rushes, that she knelt beside him.

"Are you in great pain?" she asked.

"Poor Dermot can't talk since the musket ball struck him," the widow told her."I begged him not to leave me but sure you know how stubborn young men are. 'Do you want me to be pointed out as a coward, mother?' he said. So off he went with his reaping hook to join the others and that evening – God and His Holy Mother protect us from evil – they brought him back to me on a litter. The poor crathur hasn't spoken a word since."

Úna held the young man's hand while his mother with quiet resignation recounted all that he had suffered. On hearing this Úna asked me in English to give them some money. I took out a few pence, whereupon Úna demanded that I give twenty times that amount, telling me she knew well Teige had furnished me with plenty back in Sligo.

"To buy food and shelter for you," I whispered, extracting a shilling from my purse, "not to bestow it on every needy person we meet."

But she was implacable, so I ended up giving the widow more than half our store of money, for which she called down the blessings of Saints Patrick, Colmcille and Brigid on our heads. She begged us to wait till she had warmed up an *aigen* of *praiseach*. It was with difficulty we convinced the good woman we had already eaten and, accompanied by our guide, took our leave.

Once we were outside, Úna upraided me for my lack of generosity. "Are you always so tightfisted in Tirerrill?" she mocked.

"Since we're not lords of the territory like the MacDermots, we have to toil from morning till night just to keep food on the table," I retorted, "and, anyway, I wasn't saving the money for myself but for you."

This reply struck home and touching my arm like a contrite child she begged forgiveness. "I'm too ready to judge," she declared. "Can we be friends again?"

For answer I wanted to take her in my arms and kiss her. Instead I heard myself say: "Yes, little prodigal princess! We're both just worn out from travelling."

Having been warned that Tulsk was strongly garrisoned we avoided it next day, proceeding by way of Queen Maeve's Rathcroghan to Lislaghna, where we rested that night, snow still making travel difficult. As in Elphin and Ardcarn, the people of the house would accept no payment, declaring they were glad to help friends of the O'Conors. They told us that the previous week there had been another gathering of chieftains from all over the county in Ballintober and that it was rumoured that a large army had been sent from England to reinforce the New Gall in Athlone town. And, they assured me, Muiris O'Mulconry was still living in Ballintober – hadn't Phelim the Pedlar seen him with his own eyes only a few days previously.

When we took leave of our hosts we continued in a southwesterly direction to Knockalaghta, where we shared a griddlecake in the shelter of the empty O'Conor castle. About an hour later Ballintober came into view, a massive fortress on a low hill with the red cross of Saint George flying above its south tower and the green oak on a white field of the O'Conors above its north tower. There was smoke rising from a village at the foot of the hill and people moving about in front of the castle.

"Let's tie our banner to a long stick!" Úna's voice was full of excitement.

Dismounting by a culleen, I cut a hazel rod, to which we attached the banner with thin strips of bark. And so we rode forward with Úna carrying the saffron sun rising above its green linen hill.

ႣჃ

Chapter 28

When we reached the castle's massive entrance door flanked by round-faced towers and with a portcullis suspended above it we were challenged by two loutish guardsmen armed with swords. Holding out the banner Úna told them we had come to help them fight the New Gall, at which one of the guardsmen told her gruffly that, as the castle was overcrowded, we would have to join the other newly-arrived kernes down in the village. Úna began to argue but the guardsmen wouldn't relent.

"Can we speak to Muiris O'Mulconry?" I said. "He's a friend of mine."

On hearing this they dispatched a passing horseboy to fetch the ollave. When after a tense delay Muiris came out, looking much older with his bald crown, long white hair and beard, I was afraid he would have forgotten me. He peered at me from bloodshot eyes then exclaimed, "Ah, O'Duigenan, Cúcoigcríche's kinsman! Have you come from Castlefore to help me with my Chronicles?"

The guardsmen now signalled that we could enter, so leading our garrons, Úna and I followed Muiris into the bawn. It was like entering a crowded marketplace, men, women and children, horses, dogs, hens, ducks and geese, carts and wagons filling the spaces between two rows of thatched, lime-washed cottages. Instead of a central keep there were four large towers, one at each corner. Curtain walls stretched from tower to tower and these had a pigsty, byre, stable and other houses built against them, while the north wall had stone steps leading up to a banquette on which half a dozen musket-armed sentries were lolling, some of them casting dice.

"How am I to write with all this hubbub?" Muiris lamented as he led us to his own cottage, which was on the south side next to the smithy. "Whatever possessed me to leave the peace and quiet of Castlefore? But you haven't yet told me who this young warrior is," he added once we had entered the cell-like interior furnished with a straw pallet, some stools and a table covered with manuscripts."

"She's Úna daughter of Brian Oge MacDermot of Moylurg," I admitted, recalling what he had drummed into us in Castlefore about 'Purity of lips and of learning', but she must keep her name and parentage a secret, otherwise – "

"Ah, I thought I recognised the features!" he exclaimed. "You have your father's eyes and mouth, though, despite those clothes, no man or woman could ever match you in beauty. What brings you to Ballintober, Úna?"

Disarmed by his warm, open manner, Úna began telling him of her plan to have Hugh proclaimed King of Connacht on Carnfree. Immediately Muiris's eyes lit up. Would you believe it, he himself had the very same notion? Why, the white wand mounted on the wall above a straw Saint Brigid's cross was a replica of the rod of sovereignty his ancestors had handed to the new king during the inauguration. And the banner she had made could be used in the ceremony. There was certainly a new day dawning for Ireland. The Cootes and their ilk would be driven out like the greedy scaldcrows they were and the great families would rule again.

When I said I would have to find a place in the village where we could stay, Muiris was indignant. Wasn't there plenty of room in his cottage? He would get clean rushes from Teige the Cowherd for us to sleep on. Meanwhile I should visit the smithy, where the O'Cahan brothers would take charge of our garrons.

Leaving the pair talking like conspirators I walked next door. Ruairí and his brother, Felim, who a year earlier had left Tyrone to avoid harassment by planters, were forging pike heads on an anvil in their warm, soot-blackened workplace. We agreed that for eight pence they would see that the garrons were looked after, though with so many kernes about they couldn't vouch for their safety. They told me that, months previously, Dudley Costello and his brother Thomas had gone to fight in Ulster.

"They could be serving under Phelim O'Neill or Rory O'More," Ruairí wiped his soot-smeared brow with the back of his hand, "but wherever they are you can be sure those two warriors will be foremost in the gap of danger – talk about wild Mayo men! They'd tackle the devil himself."

When I returned to the cottage Úna was explaining to Muiris why she didn't want anyone else to know who she was: her family had tried to marry her to Sir Robert King and Thomas had deserted her when she was ill. From now on he was to say she was Úna O'Reilly from East Breifne. To my surprise Muiris readily acceded to this request. He himself had for a long time used the name Cormac O'Connellan to throw the New Gall off his track but last summer Coote's henchmen had captured him during a raid on Ballintober and imprisoned him in Castlecoote. If Hugh O'Conor hadn't freed him he would probably be dead by now.

"Why did Coote's men raid Ballintober?" I asked.

"They were hoping to arrest his lordship, Bishop Egan," Muiris explained. "They knew he sometimes stayed here. When they couldn't find him they took me as they were leaving, bad cess to them for hellhounds! Nine long, miserable months they kept me like you'd keep a hog in that fortress of theirs, then when they couldn't get me to testify against O'Conor Don they decided to send me to Lord Ranelagh in Athlone – he's their new President of Connacht. Luckily we ran into Hugh and his men at Fuerty. After a few musket balls whizzed past their ears my guards galloped off. Hugh and Con O'Rourke are now besieging Castlecoote and I pray to God they'll take it soon. Did you hear that Old Sir Charles wanted to kill every Catholic in Dublin? And that son of his is just as bad. Those foul deeds in Ulster have given them the excuse they wanted – Bad cess to our own people up there! Why couldn't they have abided by the code of the Fianna: 'pity for the weak; fight for the strong'?"

You can imagine with what interest we listened to Muiris's account of his ordeal and he to mine about the attack by Coote on Teige, Rory and me near the Shannon then Úna was relating what had happened to her after leaving Sligo.

"Well, the curse of God on those New Gall!" Muiris declared. "They treat us like wild animals so we'll show them

147

wild animals have teeth. If I were as young as you, Daibhí, it's not here I'd be today but down with Hugh at Castlecoote."

We talked about the campaign, which was getting bogged down because of the lack of siege cannon. O'Conor Don and the other chieftains had tried to get Ulick Burke, Earl of Clanrickarde, to lead the Connacht forces but he had declined; that was why we would have to hurry up the inauguration at Carnfree. Of course Calvagh might not be willing to hand the reins over to his son but if we could show him that it was a *Hugh* to whom the prophesy referred he would probably consent.

"Why don't we get Úna to do a picture of Hugh being given the white wand?" I suggested, hoping by this means to keep her away from any fighting. "There's not a better artist in the country." And I told Muiris about the pictures she had done.

Since he would be the one presenting the wand, Muiris was delighted with my proposal, assuring Úna that he would get her whatever pigments and brushes she needed. Not entirely to my surprise she balked, reminding him that it was ages since she had set eyes on Hugh.

"You could paint him as you remember him," Muiris suggested. "He won't have changed that much. What do you say, Úna?"

For answer she just shook her head.

While Muiris set about stewing pieces of beef in a skillet and clearing papers off the table before laying out wooden platters we continued to coax her. It struck me that something was festering in her since the attack, and that, even if she could no longer paint, the task of mixing oil and pigments and trying to imagine details of the inauguration might have a healing effect. She finally relented on condition that I would ride with her to Castlecoote to meet Hugh.

"You'll not do much travelling in that weather," Muiris remarked, gazing out the window at a dark curtain of falling snowflakes.

♋

Chapter 29

Whether it was that telling Muiris about the attack had brought it all back or that she was dreaming of some misfortune that had troubled her younger days, Úna kept moaning and whimpering in her sleep. My heart went out to her as I listened to the small helpless cries like those of an abandoned child coming from the pile of rushes beside me. Once she called out something that sounded like "Dada!" but might have been "Devil!" Luckily Muiris on his pallet at the opposite side of the house snored through it all. I pulled the dried calfskins that served as blankets over my head to keep out the sounds and at last from sheer exhaustion dozed off.

The grating of the tongs as Muiris combed the ashes of the fire for live coals woke me. By this time Úna was in a deep sleep so I donned my outer clothes and when I had visited the jakes in the southeast tower, where up to a score of kernes were sleeping, helped Muiris get breakfast ready. He had a small storeroom at the end of the house in which he kept food, including oatmeal, milk, potatoes and, hanging from the roof, a flitch of bacon. On finding that there was only half a griddlecake left he told me not to worry, as he would get more from the bakery later. The people were very good to him: now and again the butcher even gave him a piece of fresh meat. They all knew that he was highly regarded by the O'Conors.

"Did I tell you that young Sir Charles Coote tried to get me to write a satire on O'Conor Don?" he asked. When I shook my head he continued. "Oh, yes. I was taken from the dungeon to the Great Hall and at first after spending months in darkness the light nearly blinded me. Gradually I recovered my sight and there the black villain sat at table with two growling mastiffs beside him. 'I'm told you're a rhymer as well as a chronicler,' he remarked, offering me, who'd been given nothing but watery stirabout since I was captured, a platter of beef and bread and a goblet of wine. 'You've refused to testify against your master. A pity – though I can understand such loyalty... But would you consider penning a lampoon on him? You could write it in Gaelic and no one need know who composed it – something about a drunken sot who styles himself heir to the kings of Connacht. In return, you'll be given your freedom.'

'Since you don't speak Gaelic, how will you know it's a lampoon?' I decided to find out how far he was prepared to go.

'Oh, that'll be easy,' he replied. 'If it's not, we'll just break your fingers.'

'I could no more satirise O'Conor Don than I could eulogise a *bodach* like yourself,' I declared.

'Then the greater fool you,' he sneered, 'throwing away your liberty for a knave who can't even protect you.' And with that he signalled to his henchmen to march me back to the dungeon and gave the platter of food to the dogs without allowing me to swallow even so much as a mouthful. The curse of God on the black, heartless villain!"

"Have you done much work on the Chronicles since then?" I enquired.

"Don't mention those!" He made a wry face. "I had completed the story of the *Síol Muireadaigh* from the time of *Míl Espane,* past the reign of Rory, the last High King, and the coming of the Old Gall, down to the time of Cathal Red Hand O'Conor and, curse of God on them, didn't Coote's men the day they dragged me off burn this place to the ground. Every last sheet I'd written – not to mention my books – gone up in flames! I've tried to recall what I set down but how can I with all that's happening? That's why I believe it was God's providence that sent you here. With a clear-headed young scholar like you to assist me – " He broke off as Úna woke.

"Where am I?" she mumbled sitting up, her pale-yellow hair tumbling over her face.

"You're in the last stronghold of the Kings of Connacht," Muiris said. "How did you sleep?"

"Oh, it's you, Muiris." The hunted look left her eyes. "I thought at first I was back in Fermanagh or Sligo."

"Put those places out of your head," he told her. "You'll be safe from now on. Daibhí and I will go to the storeroom while you dress and then I'll take you to the garderobe in the Old Tower. It's on the upper floor – You may as well come with us too, Daibhí."

In no time we were trudging through the snow past the physician's house, the bakery and the buttery to the large, gloomy tower, where maids were already at work in the ground floor kitchen. Muiris led the way up a winding stairs to the Great Hall. This was larger than the one in MacDermot's castle and had the O'Conor oak tree carved in the stone above the fireplace. A long table occupied most of the flagged floor with a smaller table set crosswise at its end, before a narrow, mullioned window. A threadbare Flemish tapestry of knights and ladies at a tournament covered the back wall, against which an oak settle had been placed.

"The servants, kernes and field workers eat here," Muiris explained. "I join them for Sunday dinners, unless the O'Conors invite me to the New Tower. Seeing that tomorrow's Shrove Tuesday we'll come here. There'll be great feasting on beef and ale before Lent starts – not that I've the stomach now for such things."

When we had surveyed the Hall, he led us down a low passageway to the garderobe then, leaving Úna, he and I climbed the stairs to the next floor where we peeped into the servants' bedroom. On Úna joining us, Muiris as a favour to her showed us the room where Bishop Egan stayed during his visits.

"Is it true he goes round disguised as a merchant?" she asked, looking at the canopied bed, scrubbed floor and table with sheets of writing paper.

"Yes." He smiled. "You and he have much in common."

If I had made that remark, Úna would have taken offence but now she just said, "I only dress like this because it makes it easier to walk and ride."

151

"And why shouldn't you?" he approved. "In olden times didn't our women fight alongside the warriors – not that I'm saying you should imitate them?"

Instead of walking straight back to the cottage Muiris, at Úna's request, led us past a postern gate in the west wall to the New Tower, which had been rebuilt in Twenty Seven. It was more ornate than the other towers and stood at the northwest corner. No smoke was rising from the chimney. Since there was nobody about we continued on past the weaver's cottage, intending to make a full circuit of the bawn. To our surprise we saw a frail, neat-bearded man wearing a rich, brown woollen cloak and plumed hat standing in the snow, gazing up at the banquette. It was O'Conor Don. When we reached him he turned around with a distracted look on his face.

"You're out early, Sir," Muiris greeted him.

"Oh, it's you, O'Mulconry." He spoke with a soft, cultured accent. "And who are these young people?"

We introduced ourselves, Úna telling him she was the daughter of Owen O'Reilly from Cavan. He welcomed us warmly enough, though it was clear his mind was elsewhere.

"Look at that!" he exclaimed. "Not one sentry on the banquette. If a raiding party rode down from Abbeyboyle or up from Athlone we'd be caught off guard. They're probably thinking that the snow will keep us safe but they don't know what they're up against. If only Hugh or Charles were here to impose discipline..."

"Daibhí and Úna came all the way from Sligo to help us," Muiris said. "They can tell you how our people routed the New Gall there."

"I know about Sligo," he shrugged. "It was a good victory but apart from the abbey and two strong houses the town had no real defences. Down here we haven't the cannon and muskets to take Elphin and Roscommon, never mind Athlone. Why, we don't even have the weapons to defend ourselves. The O'Cahans tell me they haven't enough iron left to make any more pikes so unless we use our ploughshares for iron we'll be at the mercy of any besieger. Do you realise that in the last war Red Hugh O'Donnell breached these walls in a few hours by placing a single Spanish cannon over there on Ballyfinegan Hill?"

"It may be true that we lack cannon and muskets," Úna blurted out, "but we'll get them by seizing them from our enemies. If we have enough men prepared to fight we can starve the Cootes and the Kings and the Hamiltons into submission."

"Who is this warrior princess?" O'Conor looked at her in amazement.

"She's somebody who has come to help us," Muiris reminded him. "Wait till you see the beautiful banner she made – it shows the sun rising above a green hill. And she's going to paint a picture of an inauguration on Carnfree."

"These are fine things," O'Conor Don waved them aside, "but we need muskets, not pictures and banners. Still, I suppose they'll do no harm. We can talk about them later." And nodding vaguely, he plodded off to the New Tower.

"That man has too many troubles weighing him down," Muiris observed as we continued our walk. "I didn't want to add to them by telling him that it's his son, Hugh, we'll have in the inauguration picture."

❧

Chapter 30

Luckily snow remained on the ground for the first two weeks of Lent, in which time Úna became engrossed in her newest work of creation. Hugh's brother, Charles, had returned from escorting Bishop Egan to the Burke castle in Glinsk, where he would be less open to capture. On meeting Úna, Charles, a bright-faced, eager young man of twenty, with brown hair and a long, slightly aquiline nose, had fallen under her spell, readily agreeing to ride back to Glinsk to obtain paints and brushes. Now, when not helping his father improve discipline among the guardsmen, he was standing in for Hugh, as Úna, brow creased in concentration, studied his face before transferring its image, brushstroke by brushstroke, to a wooden panel propped up on the table. Meanwhile Phelim the Weaver with the help of his wife and daughters had begun to fashion sun banners like the one we had brought from Sligo.

In order to repay Muiris for his hospitality I made a fair copy of the opening chapter of the Chronicles and helped him compose new ones. Úna borrowed half a dozen sheets of our paper in order to write a long letter to her brother Teige, which she proceeded to do whenever she grew tired of painting. So it was that despite alarms and preparations for defence our cottage became an island of peaceful labour. On Sundays we ate dinner in the Old Tower, though Úna often grew nervous if the men, fascinated by her doublet and wide-brimmed hat, stared openly. Muiris told them she had to dress like this in Breifne to avoid attack by Planters, an explanation that drew murmurs of sympathy, in particular from the O'Cahans.

"Did you hear that Hugh O'Neill's nephew, Owen Roe, is said to be coming back from the Netherlands?" Ruairí asked. "He'll train us to fight properly."

"Aye," Felim added, "the bible-praters will find their day is finished."

"Not if we haven't the weapons they have," Niall the Cobbler, a hunchback with a keen mind and great fund of stories, remarked. "Words never won battles."

On hearing this Úna pushed her platter with its half-eaten salted herring and griddlecake away and rose.

"Where are you going?" I asked.

"To Castlecoote," she said, "where I should have gone weeks ago."

It was with difficulty Muiris and I persuaded her to sit down till we had finished eating. Once back in the cottage she wanted to destroy the painting.

"You can't do that!" Muiris was indignant. "There's been nothing done to equal it since I came to Ballintober. It'll be a wonder to everybody here."

"But that's not even Hugh's face," Úna pointed out.

"It's close enough," Muiris said. "Wait till O'Conor Don sets eyes on it! Why, you've shown me just as I am, white head and all."

We finally convinced her that she should leave the painting till she had seen Hugh then change it if she wished. It was much harder to keep her from setting out for Castlecoote right away, now that the last of the snow had melted. When I refused to go she stormed out and asked Charles. After he agreed, I decided against my better judgment to accompany them in the morning.

That evening Úna and I walked down past a small roofless church and graveyard to the village, a collection of windowless cabins fronting an open space where kernes armed with staffs and miodoges were carousing around blazing fires. There was one two-storied alehouse built with timber and mortar like those in Sligo and with a painted gold meadar hanging above the door. The O'Cahans had told me that its landlord, O'Beirne, was looking after our garrons.

When we walked into the alehouse it was full of kernes drinking, smoking and playing cards by the feeble light of a few candles. O'Beirne, his round, red face perspiring, brought us two meadars of claret, for which he charged a halfpenny. He assured me that our garrons would be outside next morning. After some bodachs began pressing close to ogle Úna we swallowed our claret and retreated from the noisome den into the cool air outside. They dogged our footsteps uphill and, when we neared the graveyard, one of them called out that the good-looking youth would be better off with him than with a cripple like me.

At this another guffawed, "Don't forget us, Slasher!"

"You'll all have your turn," Slasher assured them.

Úna whimpered like a frightened animal. Knowing that she was reliving what had happened in Sligo, anger replaced my fear. On that occasion she had been set upon by New Gall, now it was our own kernes that were bent on despoiling her. Telling her to keep walking, I waited till the half dozen or so bodachs had come abreast of me then as they were about to attack I called out in a calm voice, "*Dominus vobiscum.*"

My use of Latin puzzled them so that they hesitated, though the tallest bodach, an ogre whose wolfish voice proclaimed him to be Slasher, put his arm tightly about my neck almost choking me and demanded to know what I had said.

"*Dominus vobiscum,*" I repeated. "*Misereatur tui omnipotens Deus, et dismissis peccatis tuis*: may Almighty God have mercy on you and forgive you your sins."

"Are you a priest?" the bodach asked, his ale-sodden breath almost making me retch.

"No, a lay brother," I raised my hand in warning, "but that young man you're following is an ordained Franciscan. He has just returned from Louvain to assist his Lordship, Bishop Egan, with his pastoral work. I'm his clerk."

"If he's a priest, what was he doing in an alehouse?" Though he loosened his arm my captor was still suspicious.

"He was used to taking wine with his meals in the Netherlands," I explained. "It's the custom among our students there. We didn't wish to give scandal in O'Beirne's by wearing our habits. Now I'm sure you're all good Christians, so *Dictum sapienti sat est*: a word to the wise is sufficient."

"By the tooth of Saint Patrick we never knew what he was," the ogre mumbled, releasing my neck. "Did we, men?"

"No, we didn't!" his comrades declared.

"Call the father back," Slasher urged, "and I'll go down on my knees and – "

"There's no need for that," I hastily assured him, again raising my hand, "*Benedicat vos omnipotens Deus*", and with this blessing I turned on my heel and limped briskly away. I could hear the kernes arguing among themselves as they moved back downhill. Would God punish me for my blasphemous lies?

"What did you say to them?" Úna asked when I caught up with her.

"Just a few Latin phrases Father Malachy taught me," I told her. "I convinced them you're a priest back from Louvain."

"And what will happen when they find out I'm not?" She glanced over her shoulder to make sure we weren't being followed.

"We can cross that ditch when we come to it," I said.

"Oh, Daibhí, I was scared," she confessed. "I was certain they..." her voice trailed off. "You were really brave."

"Oh, there was no real danger," I tried to hide my pleasure. "As the proverb has it, 'He who isn't strong has to be crafty.' Those bodachs didn't even draw their miodoges. Are you alright now?"

For answer she kissed me lightly on the cheek and we finished our walk to the castle in companionable silence.

The sun was rising above the low eastern hills when Úna and I after a restless sleep rode from the village with Charles, who was mounted on a lively saddle horse. He was armed with a sword and musket, while Úna had a pistol and I a miodoge. We reached Oran in little more than an hour then headed for Dunamon. Úna wishing to avoid Turlough's wife's family, the MacDavid Burkes, would not agree to enter the castle, so once we had crossed the River Suck by the castle bridge we continued southward, eventually running into a foraging party of kernes, who told us that Hugh and the rest of his men were encamped near Creggs.

"Why aren't they at Castlecoote?" Charles asked in surprise.

" They're trying to round up cattle," the leader explained. "We've used up most of our supplies. O'Rourke's men are keeping the castle surrounded."

Now that we knew where to go we quickened our pace, fording a small river and keeping it on our right as we approached the hills ahead. We hadn't gone many furlongs when the sound of pistol fire reached us. Only pausing while Charles and Úna primed their guns and lit their slow matches, we urged our tired mounts to greater speed. Mingling with the sound of shots we could hear faint yells and curses, some in English. The clamour grew louder as we made our way onto higher ground. Presently a longhaired kerne came running towards us, blood streaming down his face.

"What happened?" Charles demanded.

"Horse soldiers!" he cried. " The whoresons caught us off guard."

"Is Hugh all right?" Charles asked but the kerne just kept running.

If we hadn't stopped her Úna would have galloped forward. It was well she didn't for presently a body of horsemen appeared on the skyline, cantering in a close mass. We hid behind some whitethorns, hoping they hadn't seen us. As they drew closer I could make out the tall, leading rider with sombre clothes and black, broad-brimmed hat: it was Young Sir Charles Coote. His men had a prisoner with them.

As soon as the horsemen were out of sight we hurried on. The scene that met our eyes on crossing the hill filled us with dismay: bodies strewn before a few trampled sod-and-branch shelters erected near the river, an ox carcass toppled from a spit onto a smouldering fire, ravens and scaldcrows already arriving. When we rode into the encampment we saw that the bodies were covered with gore from sword wounds; some had been shot in the face. We counted fourteen in all. Luckily Hugh wasn't among them, but Charles found his wide-brimmed beaver hat beside a fallen shelter.

"They've captured him," Úna cried. "What will they do to him?"

Charles was too stunned to answer so I said: "They'll probably keep him as a hostage. He's too valuable to kill."

"What's to be done now?" She looked at me distracted. "He was going to free us. I even brought the banner – Oh, this is an ill omen. And those poor men; butchered like cattle – I can't bear to look at them."

"We'll wait here till some of the foraging parties return." I spoke with more decisiveness than I felt. "We can get them to bury the bodies. Then we'll send some of them to Ballintober with – "

"You can wait," Charles roused himself. "I'm going to Castlecoote."

Since his mind was made up, I reluctantly followed him and Úna. We hadn't gone more than a mile, however, when we ran into a rider sent by Con O'Rourke to warn any of Hugh's men he encountered that the siege was over.

"Did you see Hugh before you left?" Charles demanded.

"Yes," the man said. "We saw him being led into the castle but we couldn't fire our muskets for fear of hitting him. Anyway, most of our men were scattered."

"If only you hadn't talked me out of coming yesterday," Úna said bitterly, looking at me.

ℭℬ

Chapter 31

That was the beginning of a series of misfortunes that befell us. Because our horses were too tired to travel, we repaired one of the shelters and, despite the bodies of the slain still lying unburied outside, spent the night in it. Next morning when – God forgive us for allowing hunger to make us ignore our Lenten duty – we were eating some of the roasted ox, Úna felt sick, so that in order to have the O'Conors' physician examine her we decided on an early departure.

When we reached Ballintober the news of Hugh's capture caused universal gloom. O'Conor Don and his wife, Lady Mary, were disconsolate. If Charles hadn't argued against it they would have offered to disband the kernes provided Coote freed their son. As it was they wrote to Sir Charles assuring him of their loyalty to the king and pleading for compassion. About this time a band of foragers who hadn't fled to their own homes arrived from Creggs with one of Con O'Rourke's captains. This man informed us that it was the sudden descent of a troop of horse led by Sir Robert King that had scattered the besiegers around Castlecoote. While Sir Robert held the castle, Coote had led a raiding party to Creggs. In the aftermath Con O'Rourke had decided to return to North Leitrim, where his own people were under threat from the Hamiltons.

Owen the Physician, whose cottage was beside Muiris's, told Úna that, while her speech showed her to have been gently raised, she had been enduring hardships fit only for men; if she didn't rest she might not regain her strength. Coming after the shattering of her dream of proclaiming Hugh King of Connacht this warning did little to raise her spirits. She was often sick in the morning and during the day would sit in a corner half dressed, toying with her uncombed locks. We had hidden the painting in the storeroom for fear she would destroy it and tried to get her to take the herbal drinks that Owen made up.

"Why don't you ask him for *gafann* so that I can sleep?" she would complain.

161

"He said you're to take this." I would hold out a brimming spoon.

"You're as cruel as father was," she would grumble before swallowing.

"Why do you always blame your father?" I asked on one occasion.

"Haven't I good reason?" She looked at me distraught. "How could he love that woman more than his own flesh and blood?"

"What woman?" I did not conceal my surprise.

"Margaret Burke or, rather, DeBurgo!" She almost spat.

"But she was his wife," I remonstrated, "and she's your mother."

"Oh, what's the use of talking to you?" She pushed me angrily away.

On top of everything Muiris found that he couldn't make any progress with the Chronicles. Try as he might the storm clouds gathering over Connacht made his recording of past happenings seem a waste of time.

"Look at the years spent on *The Annals of the Kingdom of Ireland* and where are they now?" he lamented. "I worked on them myself for a month above in Donegal and so for two and a half long years did my kinsman, Fearfasa, and your own kinsman, Cúcoigcríche. Labour in vain. The New Gall are printing books by the score, aye by the hundreds, in Dublin and London but who will print ours?"

Weeks went by without any message from the Cootes or any appearance of an escape from our difficulties. It was during this time that I began to recite for Úna those Fenian tales I had gathered in the hope of cheering her up. *The Pursuit of Diarmuid and Grainne* became her favourite. She would listen intently to the adventures of the lovers as they fled across Ireland, evading Finn and his warriors. I tried to put off describing the hunt on Ben Bulben where Diarmuid is killed by the wild boar but, sensing my reluctance, she demanded to hear it. Accordingly, I related what had happened up to where Grainne makes her lament over her

162

husband's body and pretended that was all, but she was not to be hoodwinked.

"What happened after that?" she demanded, so, reluctantly, I told how, after a period of conflict, Grainne had consented to marry Finn.

"Surely you won't write down that ending?" she remarked. "You should have her die of grief."

"It's how I heard the story recited," I said.

"But those stories often have more than one ending," she cleverly pointed out. "Couldn't you have her killing herself after her marriage to that vengeful old schemer, just like Deirdre did after her marriage to King Conor?"

"You're asking me to ignore what I've heard from Blind Ciaran in Sligo and from shanachies in Galway," I protested. "I must tell the story as it was told to me."

"Oh, you're just a mere scribe then," she mocked and from that time on would listen to no more of my Fenian tales.

To avoid sinking into a slough of despond I discussed with Charles the possibility of proclaiming his father King of Connacht. He jumped at the notion, especially as the O'Conor Roes, the O'Flynns and others were now besieging Athlone without having consulted O'Conor Don.

"I was intending to join the besiegers myself," Charles said, "but if we can get father to agree to the inauguration it will bring all Connacht together."

Having got Charles's support, I next broached the idea to Muiris. At first he was hesitant, citing the prophecy's mention of Hugh, but at last accepted that further delay would only breed disunity. O'Conor Don balked also until Charles persuaded him that the inauguration could be carried out quietly so as not to endanger Hugh's life. After that preparations went ahead at a rapid pace. It was decided that the best time would be Easter Monday, when everyone would be feeling hopeful after the forty-day Lenten fast. Accordingly, invitations were sent to all the neighbouring chiefs, including Turlough MacDermot; Charles rode to Glinsk, where Bishop Egan agreed to participate, and a

163

messenger was sent to the Archbishop of Tuam, Dr. Malachy Queely, but that great champion of freedom was at the time unable to travel because of an ague. Nevertheless, he gave our plan his blessing.

In that year, as Muiris explained, Pope Gregory's calendar showed Easter to fall on the third Sunday in April, not the second as the New Gall maintained, but then their calendar was also ten days behind ours. To make sure that no canker of sin would blight the inauguration we were all encouraged to have ourselves shriven by a friar who arrived in Ballintober on Maundy Thursday and sat waiting for us in the Old Tower. Úna refused to go near him, telling me that God had abandoned her.

"Why do you say such a thing?" I protested.

"Because," she almost whispered, "He knows my heart is bad, so when I prayed before He didn't help me."

"Your heart's a thousand times better than mine," I assured her but she just turned away and looked at the fire as if gazing into the infernal regions.

Late on Holy Saturday Bishop Egan slipped through the postern gate but, though disguised as a merchant, word of his arrival soon spread so that early next day everybody converged on the Old Tower for Easter mass. By the time Úna yielded to my entreaties to follow Muiris out to the Great Hall it was already packed. We were therefore obliged to stand with others on the winding stairs, which, since Úna was wearing doublet and breeches, was fortunate.

At Holy Communion I managed to force my way upstairs into the crowded passage, then into the stifling hall, where the long centre table had been removed to provide more standing room. The raised table beneath the mullioned window had been turned into an altar before which Bishop Egan, dressed in a white tunic and embroidered saffron chasuble, stood. He was an ascetic looking man of middle years, whose neatly trimmed black beard was streaked with white. In due course I received the consecrated bread from the hand of His Lordship, then traced the sign of the cross on myself and withdrew. On making my way back downstairs, I found Úna on the point of collapse. There was nothing for it but to escort her to Muiris's cottage, where, having sipped some water, she lay down on her bed of rushes and closed her eyes. By the time I returned to the tower the bishop was giving the final blessing.

The inauguration was set to take place next day on Carnfree mound, which topped a hill about seven miles northeast of Ballintober and two miles south of Tulsk. To avoid detection by the English garrison in Tulsk those invited were asked to approach the hill in small groups of three or four. Muiris, Úna and I were to ride out ahead of the O'Conors, who would follow an hour later with Bishop Egan. Much to our dismay Úna was again sick in the morning.

"You and Muiris can go," she said in a listless voice. "I'll be all right."

You can imagine the warring thoughts in my head: I had been looking forward to this ritual that had been enacted on Carnfree from the time of Saint Patrick; now I could only attend it by leaving Úna behind on her own. With a heavy heart I watched Muiris go out with his white wand to join the O'Conors in the New Tower.

"You don't have to stay because of me," Úna demurred. "Go on! Why are you waiting? I've been left on my own before."

"Who left you on your own?" I tried to hide my resentment.

"Plenty of people." She gazed into the fire.

Just when I thought she would remain silent for hours she began to speak in a low voice: "We were invited to a wedding in Cuppanagh Castle: Ferghal O'Gara was getting married to Mary O'Conor, Hugh's cousin. I thought we would all be going but Dada said we would be too many for the O'Garas so all he took was the boys and mother. Honora and Margaret were in Croghan – I was left behind with Bridgeen."

"What age were you?" I asked.

"What does that matter?" She looked up.

"I was just curious." I shrugged.

165

"I don't know what age," she said. "I might have been ten or eleven. Why is it that girls are always the ones left behind? Teige was younger that me but Dada took him, probably to show him off."

"Your father used to take you with him to Galway," I reminded her.

"That was only so he could use me to soften the merchants," she said. "He didn't care how they drooled over me or tried to touch me. Once he went out and left me with Theobald Lynch, who he probably hoped would ask for my hand – I'll never forgive him for that. Never!"

"Have you ever loved any man, apart from Thomas?" I ventured to ask.

"Don't mention that flatterer's name," she snapped. "I never want to set eyes on him again. He's like all men, takes a few bites from an apple then tosses it away."

"Am I like that?" I looked offended.

"No, I suppose not," she conceded. "Daibhí, I sometimes think there's something wrong with me that won't let me love anybody. That's what makes men so determined to win me – they just can't believe my heart is turned to stone."

"You're just talking like this because you're feeling sick," I objected. "When you're better you'll be singing and laughing again."

She didn't answer, only resumed her perusal of the fire.

It was late that evening when Muiris walked in the door, his eyes gleaming.

"You should both have been there," he declared. "It was the grandest sight! All the chieftains and His Lordship, the bishop, gathered on the mound. Of course, a few that should have been taking part such as O'Flannagan and MacDockwra couldn't come, and because of the cold O'Conor Don didn't remove his clothes, just his cloak, but these were small things – Oh, and Úna, your brother and his lawyer friend, Eamonn, are beyond in the New Tower. I wasn't sure if you'd want it known you were staying here."

166

Úna didn't answer so I whispered to Muiris that we would ask Turlough to visit her later. She divined what I said and told us she didn't want to see anybody.

ॐ

Chapter 32

An hour later Úna and I were sitting by the fire listening to Muiris recount yet again the exact manner in which, after O'Conor Don had placed his foot on the inauguration stone, he, Muiris, had presented the white wand to him when there was an knock on the door. It was Turlough, at once plain and imposing in his leather jerkin and plumed hat. He explained that he had heard Charles O'Conor mention a beautiful young woman who was living with Muiris and had come, as soon as he could get away from the war council in the New Tower, to satisfy his curiosity.

The meeting between brother and sister was fraught with pent-up emotions. Once she had gotten over her surprise at his entry the two began to talk about the inauguration, though when their conversation turned to family matters, Muiris and I, on the pretext of visiting the garderobe, left. When we returned half an hour later Turlough had his arm about Úna, who was standing near the fire, sobbing.

"Everybody wants you to come back," he was saying, to which she retorted, "Maybe you and Teige do but not the others. As far as they're concerned – "

Disturbed by our entry she resumed her seat. Muiris offered to leave the cottage for another half hour but Turlough, explaining that he was expected back at the council, embraced Úna and, thanking us for all we had done, headed for the door.

"Wait!" Úna called out. "I've something for Teige." Going to a wickerwork basket in which she kept her banner and some undergarments Caitilín, the weaver's wife, had made for her she retrieved the letter written in the days before our illfated journey to Creggs. "You're not to read it," she commanded, handing it to him, " and, above all, don't let Eamonn find out I'm here."

I went out with Turlough and as we walked towards the New Tower, where the sun banner hung from a pole, he paused suddenly. "Teige told me about all you did for Úna," he said. "We owe you more than money can repay but..." He grasped my hand and tried to put a fistful of silver in it. "Here's something to see that you or she never goes hungry. Promise me that you'll always look after her."

"There's no need to pay me," I assured him. "As for looking after her, I'll do my utmost to keep her from harm, though that's like keeping a moth from a candle."

If I could have seen into the future I would have realised that with Turlough's departure the following morning Úna's last chance of being saved was eluding us, but how can you save somebody who doesn't desire it?

The proclaiming of O'Conor Don as king didn't bring much change of fortune either. Instead of a united campaign against the New Gall we heard that the Earl of Clanrickard was still refusing to throw in his lot with us, that Sir Lucas Dillon who had presided over the Christmas meeting in Ballintober had been making overtures to Lord Ranelagh, the President of Connacht, and that our troops surrounding Athlone were more successful in pillaging the countryside than in conducting the siege. To add to the general gloom there was no news of Hugh, Young Sir Charles Coote disdaining to reply to repeated letters from O'Conor Don except to tell the messenger who had delivered the last one that all captured rebels were being sent to Dublin, where they would be examined for sedition by the lords justices, Parsons and Borlase.

"How can Hugh be guilty of sedition if he's fighting on the King of England's behalf?" Charles fumed; to which I pointed out that Coote would no doubt argue that parliament not the king was the new sovereign.

During all this time Úna continued in low spirits. If I suggested returning to Cloonybrien to help Turlough organise his regiment she replied that he could do very well without her and, anyway, he had Teige to help him. If I asked her to paint another picture of the inauguration with O'Conor Don as the central person on the mound she would insist that what was broken couldn't be so easily mended. Nobody wanted her ugly pictures anyway. If I asked her to walk with me to the village she would flare up, saying she didn't want to be near those horrible kearnes with their leering faces. Would I be able to drive them off if they attacked her?

By now I should have realised that Úna's lethargy rose from something deeper than the shattering of her dream to make Hugh King of Connacht. She had suffered reversals in Fermanagh and Cavan but somehow had emerged with her spirit unbroken. Even the brutal assault on her south of Sligo had not crushed her. Why then was she surrendering to adversity after this defeat, if defeat it was?

June went by before the answer dawned on me, an answer that would have occurred to my mother or sisters months previously: Úna was with child. The only excuse I can offer for not realising this earlier is that being unmarried I knew little of women and Muiris was no less ignorant. We had not told Owen the Physician about the Sligo assault so he too was left in the dark. I must add in my own defence that sensing that she needed help I redoubled my efforts to persuade her to travel with me to Cloonybrien. When she accused me of plotting with her mother and Cathal Roe to get her once more into their clutches I gave up in despair.

At the beginning of July we received word that Sir Frederick Hamilton had attacked Sligo while the garrison was engaged in a distant expedition. His men had set the town on fire then mercilessly hacked down people fleeing into the streets. Others, including women and children, they had knocked on the head or drowned in the river. In all up to three hundred of the inhabitants had been killed before Sir Frederick and his soldiers returned in triumph to Manorhamilton.

"He'll probably claim he was avenging those people butchered in the jail by a drunken mob," I said at a meeting in the New Tower. This meeting was held on the first floor in a carpeted, wood-panelled room with a tapestry of a boar-hunting Irish chieftain hanging on the wall. Since I had been in Sligo soon after its capture Charles had invited me to join his parents, his uncles, Hugh Oge and Brian Roe, and Ruairí the Blacksmith. We

171

were seated round a cloth-covered table with O'Conor Don at its head and Lady Mary, a robust woman with the haughty manner of a duchess, ensconced in a wickerwork chair beside him. Behind them portraits of King Charles and a man in Elizabethan bonnet and ruff could be seen – was this Sir Hugh, O'Conor Don's father, who to the dismay of the people had given up his Gaelic title for a knighthood?

"Con O'Rourke swore to me that Hamilton gives thanks to God for every papist he kills," Charles declared.

"Wasn't Con himself captured in April at Newtown?" Hugh Oge asked. "They say Hamilton's men surprised him as he was besieging Parke's castle."

"We're not here to dwell on everything that has gone wrong but on how we can prepare for the next attack by the parliament's forces," O'Conor Don reminded us. "Now that Owen Roe O'Neill is returning to Ireland we'll soon have an experienced commander fighting on our side. In the meantime we'll have to find some way to improve our defences and arm our men. Ruairí, how many pikes have you and Felim made this week?"

As Ruairí began to answer a captain of the kernes rushed in to announce that Coote had broken through the besiegers round Athlone and relieved the town with provisions. Coming on top of the tidings from Sligo this news dismayed us. Having thanked the captain, O'Conor Don sat ashen faced until Lady Mary whispered something in his ear, then he said, "We will have to make up in numbers what we lack in horse soldiers, artillery, muskets and swords. Has anyone thought of how we might best do that?"

There followed a noisy discussion, Hugh Oge, whose stronghold was in Castlerea, insisting that we should seek help from the Mayo chieftains and his brother Brian Roe arguing that we should again send delegates to Clanrickard, who was a staunch ally of King Charles. I spoke too, advocating Úna's Rising Sun as the common banner.

"We'll fight under our own Green Oak banner like we've always done," Hugh Oge told me.

"Yes," his brother, Brian Roe agreed. "Isn't it enough that Calvagh has that girl's banner displayed over this tower?"

"Brian MacDonagh is flying it in Sligo." Realising that another setback for Úna seemed eminent, I plucked up the courage to champion her design. "He said it would unite the different families and baronies."

"I'm sure the O'Conors hardly need to take lessons from the chief of Tirerrill," Lady Mary sniffed.

"And much good her banner did him," Hugh Oge added.

"Wait!" O'Conor Don raised his right hand. "Muiris has great respect for this man's opinion, so maybe we too should listen to him. If each chieftain wants to keep his own banner, why, so be it. But we need a new banner that will embrace us all. Maybe the Rising Sun will change our luck – it can hardly make it worse."

 CƷ

Chapter 33

Whether it was the bright July weather or that a prophecy was being noised about concerning a great battle to be fought between Gael and Gall in which the Gael would triumph, O'Conor Don shook off his lethargy and began to act with new forcefulness. He summoned allies from all parts of the county so that the fields outside the castle were soon dotted with tents and campfires, around which kernes, young scullogues and their chieftains swarmed. The sun banner fluttered above the New Tower and the sentries on the banquette paced constantly back and forth.

As if stirred by all this activity Úna too grew more cheerful. She began to clean and cook for Muiris and often came with me on walks around the bawn to watch the O'Cahans forging pike heads or Rury the Carpenter fitting them on long ash handles. There was always a great bustle: carts arriving with pigs and hens; horseboys leading mares and foals out of the stable; maids carrying food from the buttery or bakery to the Old and New Tower; Niall the Cobbler eager to tell us one of his stories; a *geocach* singing about heroic deeds or plaintive tales of love and, towards midday, bare-footed women in shabby frieze tunics accompanied by ragged, shy-eyed children coming from the village with baskets of peas, watercress, gooseberries and eggs.

One evening as we were passing the butcher's Úna grabbed my arm to make me stop. She had seen Eamonn entering through the gate with a hard-faced, armed companion. We waited until the newcomers had led their horses to the stable then hurried back to Muiris's cottage. The arrival of these two seemed to bring back all her anxieties. She warned me to avoid them as they had come to spy on her. I told her that she was letting suspicion muddle her wits.

"No, I'm not," she insisted. "Honest Eamonn maintains he can't practise law because he won't take the Oath of Supremacy but father and I met busy, prosperous lawyers in Galway who hadn't sworn. He's pulling the wool over everybody's eyes."

175

Later that evening Charles invited me to a meeting in the New Tower at which Eamonn in his blunt fashion told the O'Conors and the neighbouring chieftains who were present that they were fools not to support parliament. What had King Charles ever done for them except appoint Wentworth to cheat them out of their estates? Had he honoured the 'Graces', those written promises on land and religion he had made? Had he even saved his friend Wentworth from execution?

"You forget that the Puritans and those who wish to crush the True Church are on Parliament's side," O'Conor Don pointed out. "Charles may not be the most trustworthy of monarchs but he's our best shield against people like the Cootes and Hamiltons."

"Well, at least you won't have to worry about Old Coote any longer." Eamonn changed tack. "Kevin the Piper heard on his travels that he was shot dead in May. It happened soon after he routed three thousand of our soldiers outside Trim."

"May he burn in hell," Charles exclaimed. "And his son with him."

Afterwards, as I was walking towards the garderobe, Eamonn caught up with me, begging me to take him to Úna. "It's just that I'll be going to Dunamon," he said. "Naturally when I heard of your fair warrior companion I knew Mairéad's family would be enquiring after her."

Recalling Úna's mistrust of this man, I suspected that he was hoping to sift her for information. Even if she refused to speak to him, he could still boast of having seen her. I shook my head: "She's recovering from an ague and won't meet visitors; Turlough will be able to tell them anything they want to know."

"In that case, what with the present turmoil, it could be months before they hear anything," he protested, adding in flattering tones: "Listen, you and I are old bedfellows. If you'll do this for me, I may be able to repay the favour."

Spurred on by Úna's repugnance, I decided to sound him out: "Look, I'm just a mere scribe who's been cast off by the

176

MacDermots and taken in here like a stray dog by the O'Conors, so how could you help me?"

"Oh, in guiding people through the thickets of the law I've made my share of friends." He grinned conspiratorially.

"I thought you only helped Turlough MacDermot with the law."

"And so I did, until he sent me away, just like he did with you – Not that I'm blaming him: in times like these there's more to be won by the strong hand than by endless appeals to the courts. That's why from now on I'm following my own path. Do you know that there are those who'd pay a scribe like yourself in silver or even gold to report what he hears and sees? And you wouldn't have to leave Ballintober."

"Who are those people?"

"Oh, just noblemen who wish to insure that the law of the land is upheld. I'd be acting on their behalf; you'd only have to write to me."

"Would they be men such as the Earl of Clanricharde and Sir Lucas Dillon?"

"I'll mention no names but you can take it that they're men of the highest honour and integrity."

So "Honest Eamonn" wanted to find out if I could be recruited as a spy! Taking care to show no surprise, I pretended that I could only write in Irish.

"That's no obstacle." He squeezed my arm reassuringly. "I can render your words into moderate English – We will of course have to devise a code."

"You want me to become a Judas then?" I pulled my arm away.

"What?" He appeared to be genuinely outraged. "You completely mistook my meaning. I simply wished to help someone whom I was foolish enough to esteem. But, since you obviously question my motives, I'll bid you farewell." Saying which, he bowed stiffly and walked back to the winding stairs.

That was the last time I talked to Eamonn. Next day, much to Úna's relief, he and his companion left Ballintober.

177

Charles, having heard my account of the previous evening's conversation, suspected that they might be bound for Castlecoote. He was, therefore, intent on having them followed but his father overruled him, convinced that if Eamonn intended to betray us he wouldn't have spoken so openly at the meeting. It was a judgment he would come to regret before the week was out.

On Saturday I persuaded Úna to ride with me through the fields to view the gathering army. What a thrilling sight it was: scores of groups, each with its own commander and banner; drummers beating out tattoos; pipers raising a shrill din; men putting up canvas tents; captains getting barefooted kearnes armed with pikes to form straight lines; a score of men shouldering ancient muskets; a party of horse soldiers riding up with a brown-robed friar in their midst; bodachs roasting sizzling sheep carcasses on spits over smoky fires and, by covered carts, women filling bowls with slices of fragrant mutton, which they handed out with meaders of ale and griddlecakes to newly arrived scullogues and ploughboys carrying clubs and sickles.

On seeing us draw near, a handsome sword-armed man with a glib of black hair and a thick, down-curving moustache doffed his helmet-like cap, which the Spanish call a montero, and bowing deeply offered it to Úna in exchange for a kiss.

"Here," she replied, "you may have mine," and, removing her hat, let her hair tumble down to her shoulders. There were gasps of admiration from the onlookers. They told us they were from *Tír Briúin* near the Shannon; their captain, the fellow on whom Úna had bestowed her hat, was Donogh O'Beirne and they were the bravest fighters in the entire army. Would Úna join their company and bring them good luck?

"Don't be foolish," I whispered, recalling what the streetwalker in Sligo had told me about O'Beirne. "They want more than good luck."

"Oh, don't be an old woman!" she retorted, her reckless spirit reviving.

I watched in dismay as she donned the montero, pushing up her tresses and pulling down the flap so that her beauty was concealed like the moon behind a cloud. The watching men greeted her transformation with groans but she told them that if she were to accompany them into battle she would have to look as fierce as they.

"Daibhí, go fetch my banner," she commanded, but I just turned silently away. Perceiving that she had offended me, she begged forgiveness in so contrite a voice that I hadn't the heart to withstand her.

As she accompanied me back to the castle, I warned her against fighting, telling her that I knew for some time she was with child.

"Then you know why I must fight," she responded, her voice emptied of hope. "Would you have me live on to become the mother of a New Gall bastard?"

"You could marry me," I declared, seizing the opportunity to reveal what was in my heart. "I would raise your child as my own and shield you with every fibre of my being. Úna, will you be my wife?"

She shook her head then looked at me with tender regret.

"You're a kind man, Daibhí," she said, "but I would only bring you sorrow." On hearing these words bitterness flooded my mind.

"I suppose a mere scribe isn't worthy of MacDermot's daughter," I observed, "especially one with a lame leg."

"No, Daibhí," she protested. "It's not that. The O'Duigenans are just as distinguished as our family, maybe more so since they're men of learning. It's just that after Thomas betrayed me I vowed I would never marry. One day you'll meet a better girl than me who will care for you and bear your children."

Her answer soothed my hurt pride, but what advice was I to give her? That she should just accept her shame? That its father's sin should not be visited on the child in her womb? At that moment I felt like screaming against the pitiless workings of fate that takes no account of beauty or the sufferings of the innocent. Why was this highborn, ardent young woman driven to believe she had no choice except that between unmerited disgrace and untimely death?

When we were in Muiris's cottage, Úna suddenly turned to me. "Daibhí," she spoke in a low, calm voice, "I didn't mean what I said about a New Gall bastard. I know that the child growing in me, whatever its flesh and blood, has a soul which came from God. That time...after the men attacked me in Sligo I wanted to die but, to my bitter shame, you found me – No, I'm not blaming you. You acted out of kindness. Since then I've grown certain that God spared me so that, like Joan of Arc and in spite of my failings, I could do something which would give our people hope. You've been a faithful companion, Daibhí, through many trials and hardships, but if you wish now to return to Kilmactranny I release you from all promises made to me or my brothers."

I shook my head and she knelt to open her wickerwork basket.

Before we arrived back with the banner the sound of bugles and bellowed commands told us something urgent was afoot. We found the scattered army trying to form itself pell-mell into battle array, while the friar we had seen earlier stood on a bank with a crucifix in his upstretched hand, calling down God's blessing on the disordered companies. A chieftain told us that a large force of New Gall from Athlone was marching up to attack us. They had already passed Oran. After much searching we spied Úna's wide-brimmed hat among the pikemen and rode over to join O'Beirne's group. Donogh was pleased with the sun banner and having consulted with other captains told us the pikemen would march behind it.

"Let me carry it," Úna begged, to which he demurred. It had amused them to consider her fit to be a soldier when there was no danger about; the imminent arrival of the enemy had changed everything. It would besmirch their honour to allow a noblewoman like her to risk almost certain death.

"That risk is mine to take, not yours to withhold," Úna snapped, grabbing the banner from the kerne holding it. "If

180

Connacht warriors followed Queen Maeve into battle surely your men can follow me?"

Heartened by this defiant speech the pikemen raised a great cheer.

"All right," O'Beirne conceded, "if you're determined to risk your life nobody will stand in your way – But all of you remember what I said."

By now another scout was galloping up to tell us that the New Gall were within a mile of Cleaboy. Once there, it would only be minutes till they reached Ballintober.
On hearing this, my palms began to sweat and my heart to thump painfully. The dead men at Creggs rose before my mind, their wounds filling me with horror. I had only a miodogue to protect myself, yet I was determined to stay with Úna though a sword or musket ball would probably end my life. She was armed with a pistol but with one hand holding the banner and the other the reins how would she be able to use it?

During all this time the confusion grew, nobody knowing whether we should advance or withdraw inside the castle walls. O'Beirne was for staying where we were till we received word from O'Conor Don, who was thought to be helping Charles get the horse soldiers in order. Then on the breeze came a faint, ominous tramping sound.

Chapter 34

Realising that the New Gall army was almost within striking distance the pikemen without waiting for the musketeers or horse began to move down into the village and on towards Ballyfinegan. Úna trotted ahead of them, the sun banner dancing on its staff above her head. I asked her to wait till we had definite orders from the O'Conors. When she ignored me I cantered back to the vicinity of the graveyard, where Charles rode down angrily to meet me.

"Why didn't those fools wait for the rest of our army?" he demanded.

"They want to attack the enemy before they expect it," I said.

"We should have taken up our position here, with the castle at our back," he fumed. "Now we'll lose any advantage we had." Turning around, he signalled to the two score or so musketeers to advance. Further back I could see his father urging the horse to get into formation. Since it was clear that the pikemen weren't going to be recalled I hurried after them, catching up with Úna and O'Beirne's men on the crest of Ballyfinegan Hill just as the New Gall army came into view, marching along the unpaved drove-road towards Cleaboy.

O'Beirne raised his hand and our side came to a halt to contemplate the compact mass of musketeers followed by men with long pikes held straight up and flanked by horse soldiers. The foreign cohorts, dressed in dark doublets and breeches, had not only their individual colours floating above them but also redcross Saint George banners as they advanced relentlessly towards us across the open, bush-dotted countryside. How that sight chilled my blood, especially when I compared the array of disciplined troops with our own legion of kearnes, scullogues and ploughboys, many of them barefooted and barechested and armed only with a club or sickle.

"Here, take this!" Úna handed me her pistol and powder horn. "It's loaded. All you have to do is prime it and light the slow match."

"How will I do that?" I protested but she wasn't listening. There was a smile playing about her lips as if what was about to happen were just a game. I looked round at O'Beirne and saw that he was uncertain whether to resume the advance or wait for the shot and horse. At this point Úna intervened.

"Attack!"she cried. "Quick! Before they prime their muskets."

My blood froze. Was I the only one there who knew she wanted to die? Next moment a piper began playing a stirring war tune and that together with Úna's impatience made up O'Beirne's mind.

Drawing his sword, he called out *"Faire!"* then started downhill, followed by his kernes and the other commanders with their clansmen. Úna led the way, the sun banner fluttering above her head and with my heart in my mouth I dropped the pistol and powder horn, knowing they would only encumber me, drew the miodoge dangling from my belt and urged my garron into a trot.

Across the sunlit, green pastureland I could see the New Gall foot forming into a square bristling with pikes, the musketeers loading and priming their weapons, the horse wheeling into position further back, while bugle notes rang out urgently. Then the unexpected happened: an officer in a plumed hat and mounted on a grey charger was clearly signalling to the troops to retreat. As the musketeers swung around to the flanks, a man in sombre clothes came riding up to argue with the officer. That commanding figure was unmistakable: it was Young Sir Charles Coote! Whatever he said must have changed the other man's mind because the army stood its ground.

That was all I could surmise before a wide stream confronted us. Luckily, our garrons bounded across as nimbly as deer, followed by a wave of men. When I raised my eyes again the distance between us and the New Gall had shrunk so much I could see the deadly barrier of pike-armed soldiers as clearly as our own troops. By now O'Beirne's kernes, led by pikemen shouting the ancient warcry *"Fág an bealach!"* had overtaken Úna and me and, undeterred by a fusillade of musket shots, were dashing headlong towards the enemy. Here and there men on either side of me began keeling over as if poleaxed but the charge continued. With a sickening feeling I saw a brute with a pot helmet raising his pikehead towards my breast. Ducking aside to avoid it my lame leg lost its grip. I tumbled from the garron's back and hit the ground with a wallop that left me gasping.

Pain seared through my shoulder and bad leg but, picking up the miodogue, I forced myself to rise. Immediately I found myself surrounded by screaming, cursing demons who were thrusting with pikes, slashing with swords, swiping with clubs and sickles and stabbing with miodogues. Úna was nowhere to be seen. A fellow with a bleeding gash on his face tried to run me through with his pike but before he could drive it home one of our scullogues felled him with a blow of his club. Another pikeman was about to slay my rescuer when I thrust my miodogue into his unguarded side. More than forty years later I can still feel the blade sinking in between his ribs. Filled with horror, I didn't withdraw the weapon but, like someone in a dream, stood there bereft of power, watching the blood ooze out. Next minute a surge of fighting men overtook me, my lame leg gave way in the crush and I collapsed under their feet. In the ensuing maelstrom I crawled alongside a dead enemy soldier and pretended to be dead too.

By now the renewed sound of musket fire could be heard clearly above the general din. I raised my head to see if our men were being hit. Somebody yanked me to my feet. It was O'Beirne, still wearing Úna's hat.

"Come!" he shouted. "They're slaughtering us like cattle."

"Where's Úna?" I asked but he just kept moving, dragging me along, thrusting at enemy soldiers with his sword. Next moment a musket ball smashed into his head, spraying his brains over my sleeve. It was at that moment I spied Úna's montero. Her garron and banner were gone. As I called out to her a yelling body of horse swept down on us. Their leader, who was wearing a breastplate and ostrich-plumed hat, felled Úna in passing with a sword blow to the neck: it was the man I had seen dancing with her and drinking to her health, Sir Robert King! When I reached her, blood was crimsoning her doublet and trickling from her mouth. Lying beside her I cradled her in my arms despite the nauseating smell of warm gore filling my nostrils.

"Dada!" she whimpered. "Dada, I'm cold...Dada I'm...."

"Hush, Úna," I told her. "I'll stay with you always; you're safe now, Úna."

As I spoke I felt a shudder convulse her, then I must have lost consciousness because when I lifted my head slightly off the ground to look about me there were only dead and wounded to be seen beyond Úna's montero, while in the distance the New Gall were pursuing our men on horseback and foot. The groans of the wounded and the stench of spilled blood and guts made my senses reel.

Knowing that as soon as the enemy came back I would be killed, I begged the lifeless Úna to forgive me, pressed my lips on her cold cheek and my doublet stained with her blood crawled away to the shelter of some blackthorns. There I lay down in an inner hollow, spreading branches and moss over me so that I resembled a half-buried log. For what seemed an eternity I hid, trying to close my ears to ever more piteous moans and cries from the field outside. Later, I heard the New Gall returning, followed by the sounds of pistol shots, cursing, sword blows and screams and, now and again, footsteps and harsh voices as soldiers circled the thicket. Finally there was silence, broken only by the croaking of scaldcrows or the far-off lowing of a bullock.

Waiting until dark, I crawled out from my hiding place and despite the pain in my leg and shoulder began to limp back across the blood-sodden, corpse-strewn ground towards Ballintober, guided by the polestar. How I managed to wade across the stream and drag myself up Ballyfinegan Hill I don't know, unless it was fear that gave me strength, the fear that the New Gall were still about, the fear that when I got back to the castle I would find it like a charnel house, the fear that Úna's ghost would seek me out for abandoning her. After I had traversed what seemed a thousand miles I heard wailing and saw fires blazing in the village. A group of women venturing out to Cleaboy to search for dead kinsmen told me the fires had been lit outdoors by people whose cabins had been burned. O'Beirne's alehouse was a pile of ashes but the New Gall had not attacked the castle.

To add to my discomfort, rain now began to fall, so shaking off exhaustion I hurried uphill past the graveyard, recalling how Charles had accosted me there before the battle began. When I finally staggered into Muiris's cottage, the first thing he asked about was Úna. On hearing she was dead, he cried out, "Oh, no!" tears filling his old, blood-shot eyes. "The poor, poor thing!" He traced the sign of the cross on himself then listened aghast to my account of what had happened.

While I washed blood from my hands and face and dried my clothes we talked about our dead companion, her painting, her compassion for the destitute, her desire to live as freely as her brothers did, her sombre moods that could suddenly give way to dazzling joy like the sun bursting through rainclouds. According to Muiris, Úna's troubles arose from her being part of a large family. "She should have been an only child – like Queen Maeve or Gráinne O'Malley," he declared. "We'll never see her like again. May her soul be at God's right hand this night."

When I asked if I should find someone to accompany me to Cleaboy to bring back her body, he insisted that I was in no state to venture out in rain and darkness and that, anyway, it would be time enough in the morning. In the meantime hadn't I better eat something? Too sick at heart to taste the griddlecake he proffered, I sipped a meadar of ale as he remarked that Charles blamed our defeat on the haste with which our pikemen had attacked without waiting for the horse and musketeers. It was government forces from Athlone under Lord Ranelagh assisted by Coote and King that had defeated us. Charles reckoned that Eamonn had informed Coote about the army we were raising. The only good thing was that the New Gall had broken off the pursuit once they reached the village, probably fearing there were hundreds of armed men waiting for them in and behind the castle.

A sudden thought struck me. "Have you the picture of the inauguration?" I asked. "We can hang it on the wall to remind us of Úna."

After searching the storeroom he returned, shaking his head. "It's gone," he said. "She must have burned it. Maybe it's as well, seeing it wasn't to her liking."

"Some day if God gives me the strength of mind to do it I'll write down her story," I vowed. "She always dreamed of leading our people to victory."

"And maybe she will," Muiris declared. "Sure isn't her sun banner still flying above the New Tower?"

ೞ

Epilogue

All that happened over forty years ago but it's still as clear to me as if it were yesterday. I've heard it said that Parliamentarians claimed that as many as six hundred of our men were killed in the Battle of Ballintober, though that is probably an exaggeration. Later when Cromwell came over here he massacred three and a half thousand men, women and children in Drogheda alone. Sometimes I think Úna was lucky not to have lived to see those days and the confiscations that followed the war. Now with James the Second on the throne it's thought the O'Conors and MacDermots may get some of their former estates restored but I've learned to be wary of English monarchs, even Catholic ones. Weren't Mary and Philip Catholics and didn't they plant Laois and Offaly?

Though our great families were brought low by the eleven years of war that followed the Ulster rising and ended with the hellish Cromwellian evictions, life for the common people dragged on hardly worse than before, a struggle to keep body and soul together lightened by the occasional *céilidhe* and feast day. Rory never returned from Cavan, perhaps because he was killed or got married, so in time Eileen resigned herself to caring for our mother and after her death, may heaven be her bed, for Philip and his wife Deirdre's five children. She still lives with them in Kilmactranny.

I never learned what happened to Thomas Costello except for a poem I once heard Kevin the Piper recite in which it was revealed that Thomas while fighting heroically in Ulster was also wooing the wife of Hugh O'Rourke. His brother Dudley served in the regiment of our present king, at that time Duke of York, in Flanders, then about eighteen years ago he was shot for harrying Lord Dillon's tenants in the Barony of Costello, the territory that once belonged to his family.

As for myself, I travelled west in April Fifty One, a year before Coote took Galway City, after which Turlough MacDermot and the Connacht chieftains finally surrendered to the Parliamentarians. From that period until Charles the Second was five years on the throne I worked as a scribe for the open-handed O'Flahertys, first in Aughnanure Castle near Lough Corrib then once more on Red Island in Lough Mask. Twenty years ago I returned to Tirerrill and settled down here in Shancough with Bebhin MacConmee, a good, hard-working woman who, when she's not looking after our house, sharpens quills, makes ink and keeps my finished manuscripts in order. We have no children but, God willing, the many stories from our Gaelic past that I have written down may preserve my memory when this body returns to dust.

For me, apart from the shooting of Donogh O'Beirne at Ballintober, the one death from those days that haunts me is that of Úna. Maybe there's guilt in it too, my failure to protect her? During all the time I knew her I only kissed her once and that was when she was lying dead in my arms. If she had only realised how much she was loved perhaps she might not have sought the end that befell her – And despite all her changing moods, she was loved; not just by Thomas and me but, I've come to believe, even more so by her father. O'Conor Don showed me a poem Brian Oge had composed a few days before he died in Athlone.

"I would have given it to her," he explained, "only that Muiris warned me not to reveal that I knew who she was. I was in Athlone myself at the time. We had called a meeting of the chieftains to decide what we would do if Wentworth went ahead with his plantation scheme and it was just after a wild January night. Brian Oge told me he hadn't slept a wink because he thought he could hear Úna sobbing quietly to herself in the next room just as she had once sobbed as a child when he had taken away her pet fox – I think it had bitten her mother's hand so he

190

had his steward bring it out to the woods and leave it there. In the morning he wrote some ranns about it."

Opening a drawer he took out a sheet with neat old-fashioned writing that I recognized from Brian Oge's last letter to Úna. The poem went as follows:

Wind blows all night through
Blows leaves away
Blows rough blows long
Blows stars away
Wind blows to and fro
Tosses thoughts to and fro
Blows my rest away.

Wind blows all dawn too
Blows trees away
Blows tough blows strong
Blows sun away
Wind blows high and low
Tosses roof tops high and low
Blows my life away.

"Isn't it strange," O'Conor Don remarked, "that it was in Athlone her father died and it was an army from Athlone that was responsible for her own death?"

I would like to be able to state that Úna was buried in Clonmacnoise beside the father she both hated and loved but it is only in fairy tales that things end happily. When we searched the battlefield next day we couldn't find her body. Perhaps the New Gall had removed it before they withdrew or perhaps wolves had devoured it, for wolves were still plentiful in those days. A legend grew up that she had been buried in Trinity Island in Lough Key at the time Honora died and that is where to this day most people believe she lies. What does it matter where her body is so long as her spirit still haunts us with its vision of a beauty that is at once tragic and wild?

191

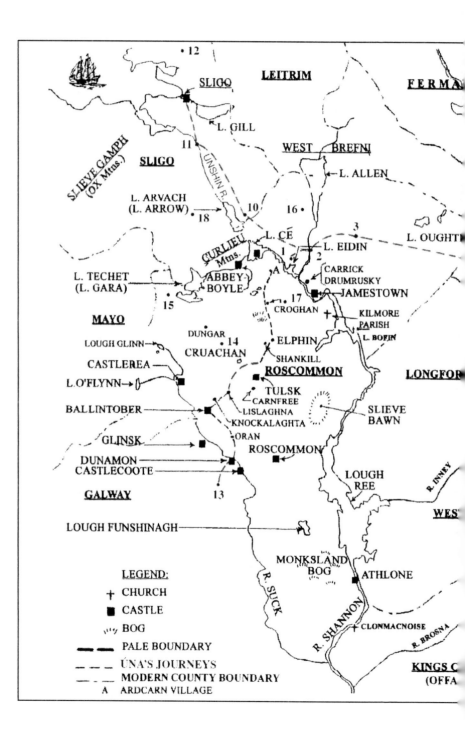

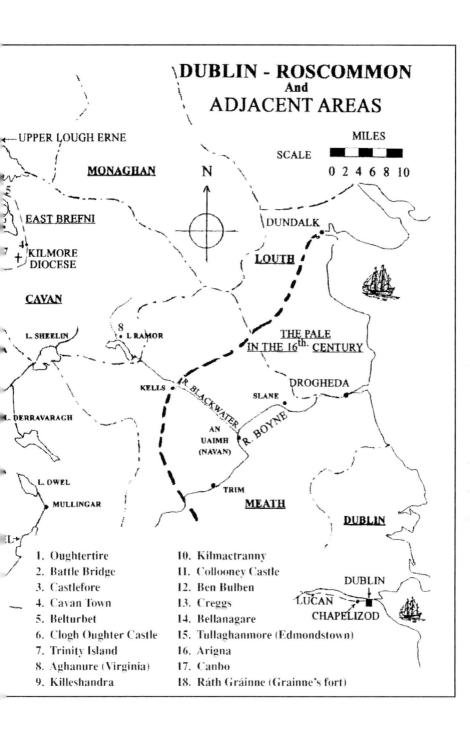

DUBLIN - ROSCOMMON
And
ADJACENT AREAS

MILES

SCALE

0 2 4 6 8 10

UPPER LOUGH ERNE

MONAGHAN

N

DUNDALK

EAST BREFNI

KILMORE
DIOCESE

LOUTH

CAVAN

L. SHEELIN

8

L RAMOR

THE PALE
IN THE 16th. CENTURY

DROGHEDA

KELLS

R. BLACKWATER

SLANE

L. DERRAVARAGH

AN
UAIMH
(NAVAN)

R. BOYNE

L. OWEL

TRIM

MULLINGAR

MEATH

DUBLIN

1. Oughtertire
2. Battle Bridge
3. Castlefore
4. Cavan Town
5. Belturbet
6. Clogh Oughter Castle
7. Trinity Island
8. Aghanure (Virginia)
9. Killeshandra
10. Kilmactranny
11. Collooney Castle
12. Ben Bulben
13. Creggs
14. Bellanagare
15. Tullaghanmore (Edmondstown)
16. Arigna
17. Canbo
18. Ráth Gráinne (Grainne's fort)

DUBLIN

LUCAN

CHAPELIZOD

Key Dates

1585	The Composition of Connacht: Gaelic titles and system of land ownership abolished
1594-1603	Rebellion of O'Neill and O'Donnell ("The Nine Years War")
1601	O'Neill and O'Donnell defeated at Kinsale (3 Jan 1602 new style)
1603	James VI of Scotland becomes James I of G.B.
1607	Hugh O'Neill and Rory O'Donnell leave Ireland ("Flight of the Earls")
1608–10	The Plantation of Ulster
1617	Sir John King is granted the lands of Boyle Abbey; Brian Oge MacDermot is granted some of his ancestral lands, including Carrick MacDermot, and Sir Hugh O'Conor Don receives a new grant of Ballintober.
1625	Charles I succeeds his father, James I, as King of England
1626	Dr Boethius Egan, a Franciscan, appointed Bishop of Elphin
1627	Charles I offers Irish Catholics concessions ("The Graces") in return for subsidies
1632	Wentworth (Lord Strafford) appointed as Viceroy in Ireland
1633	Wentworth arrives in Ireland
1634	Charles I repudiates "The Graces"
1635	Wentworth arrives in Connacht to lay the foundation for a plantation scheme – commission sits at Boyle in July
1636	Annals of the Four Masters (*Annála Ríoghachta Éireann*) completed; Brian Oge MacDermot, Lord of Moylurg, dies in Athlone - Daibhí O'Duigenan helps write his obituary?
1638	The Scots revolt against Charles I

1639-41	The last Irish parliament (save1689) in which Catholics sit; Sir Robert King represents Boyle
1640	Don Eugenio (Owen Roe) O'Neill wins praise for his defence of Arras; Strafford arrested in November
1641	Strafford executed in May; Irish rebellion begins in October; planters massacred in the North; Rory O'More defeats government forces at Drogheda; Roscommon gentry meet in Ballintober at Christmas and take oath to support the king and maintain the Catholic faith; Con O'Rourke and Hugh O'Conor besiege Castlecoote – O'Conor is captured (1642 new style)
1642	Civil War begins in England. Sir Frederick Hamilton captures Sligo; its inhabitants massacred. Owen Roe O'Neill arrives in Ireland. Battle of Ballintober: an Irish army assembled by Calvagh O'Conor Don defeated by Parliamentarians under Lord Ranelagh, Sir Charles Coote Jnr and Sir Robert King
1645	Muiris O'Mulconry ("The light of poetry"), who assisted The Four Masters for a month with their Annals, dies
1649	Cromwell begins his campaign to "pacify" Ireland; sieges of Drogheda (Sept) and Wexford (Oct)
1651	Cromwellians, under Sir Charles Coote Jnr, blocade Galway. Daibhí O'Duigenan in the O'Flaherty castle at Aghnanure, Co Galway, and later in Tadhg Oge O'Flaherty's castle, Red Island, Lough Mask.
1660	Restoration of Charles II
1696	Daibhí O Duigenan dies

Glossary

Aigen of *praiseach*: An oven (*oigheann*) of thin porridge or gruel

Baile na Carraige: The Town of the Rock

Bodach: A churl; lout

Bréidín: Homespun woolen cloth

Brehon (*breitheamh*): An Irish lawgiver and judge

Cailleach: old woman; hag

Céilidhe: an evening gathering with merriment

Ciseán: wickerwork basket

Corp: Body – here *text*; *Tochmhairc*: Wooings, courtships

Crios: A girdle; belt

Culleen (*coillín*): A little wood, often of hazel

Dé Danann: from *Tuatha Dé Danaan*, "people of the goddess Dana"

Eibhlín a Rún: Eveleen My Darling (A traditional song)

Fág an bealach! ; Get out of the way! (A war cry)

Fainic! : Beware!

Faire! : Look out! (A war cry)

Fubún! : Shame!

Gafann: Henbane

Gall: Foreigner; New Gall= New English; Old Gall= Anglo-Normans

Garron (*gearrán*): A small horse; a gelding; a nag

Geis: Binding injunction; taboo

Geocach: A strolling musician or singer

Glib: A fringe of hair over forehead, loose tress of hair

Goirm thu! : Well done, bravo!

Kerne (*ceithearn*): A lightly armed footsoldier (Woodkerne = outlaw)

Loodramawm (*Liúdramán*): A lanky, lazy person

Meadar: A wooden drinking-cup with four handles

Míl Espane: Milesius of Spain, legendary ancestor of the Irish

Miodoge (*miodóg*): A dagger

Ollave (*Ollamh*): A man learned in poetry, law, history etc.

Praiseach bhuí: Wild mustard, charlock,

Raiméis: Nonsensical talk; nonsense

Rann: A verse; stanza

Rath Dé ort: God prosper you

Reachtaire: A man in charge of a noble household; chief steward

Róisín Dubh: Little Black Rose (A poetic name for Ireland)

Sasanach: An Englishman

Sciathán: A wickerwork tray

Scollop (*Scolb*): Looped stick for securing thatch

Scullogue (*scológ*): A farmer; yeoman

Shanachie (*seanchaí*): A traditional storyteller

Shebeen (*Síbín*): A rough, country alehouse

Síol Muireadaigh: Muiredach Muillethan's decendants, e.g. O'Conors

Skean (*scian*): A knife

Sláinte: Health; *Sláinte agus saol fada*: Health and long life

Slanus (*Slánlus*): Plantain (A herb)

Spalpaire: A big strong fellow; a loudmouth

Súgán: straw rope

Tír na nÓg: The Land of the Young (One of the Celtic heavens)

Troander: Whey made by mixing buttermilk with heated fresh milk

Usquebagh (*uisce beatha*): Whiskey; literally "water of life"